THE WITCH AT THE EDGE OF THE WOOD

LIZ DELTON

Tourmaline & Quartz Publishing LLC
P.O. Box 193, North Granby, CT 06060 USA
www.LizDelton.com

Three is the most magical number.
You'll find it in the beginning, middle, and end.
You'll find it balancing the legs of a stool.
You'll find it in the morning, noon, and night.
And if you seek it often enough,
you'll find the magic in it.

TRANSLATED FROM THE FAERŬN RECORDS
PRESERVED IN THE MUSEUM AT VILLIKRY

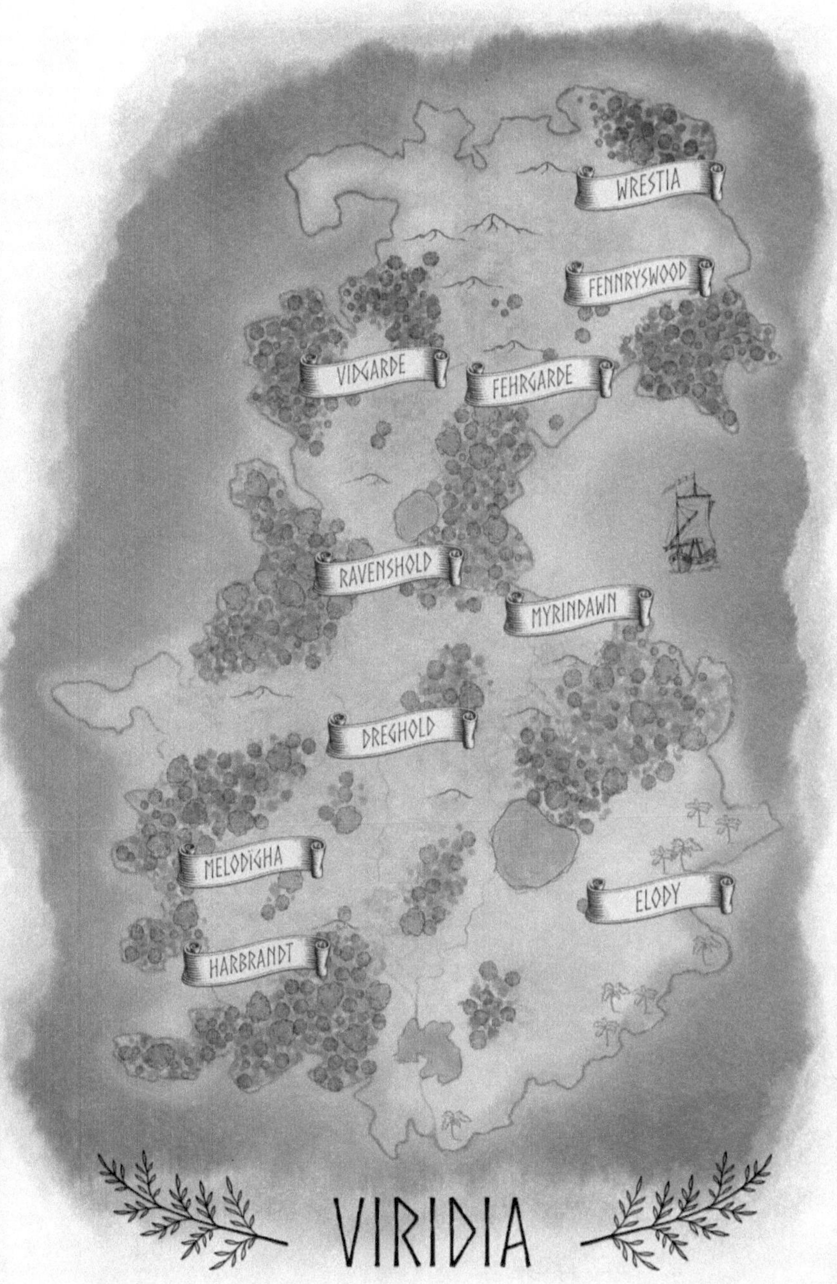

WRESTIA
FENNRYSWOOD
VIDGARDE
FEHRGARDE
RAVENSHOLD
MYRINDAWN
DREGHOLD
MELODÏGHA
ELODY
HARBRANDT
VIRIDIA

ACT I
THE
WOOD

Brambles scratched Velina's legs as she bolted through the thicket outside the Darkwood. "It has to be around here *somewhere*."

But this was the second time she'd passed a boulder shaped eerily like a skull, and she had yet to stumble upon the place she sought.

The witch should be here.

Velina had traded her last meal at the workhouse for a scrap of paper with a map scribbled on it—though the word "map" was a generous way to describe the trader's depiction. She'd stuffed the scrap of paper into her threadbare pocket and now pulled it out to study it. Crude details had been scratched with a bit of charcoal—a lump to represent the hill, a squiggle for the riverbed, a circle for the skull boulder, and a square for the witch's cottage. But the cottage wasn't here.

Had she gambled everything on a fairytale? Would she have to drag herself back into Drěghold's mucky streets and over the rotting threshold of the workhouse once again? Eghrŭn would flog her on sight for running away—then again, the orc didn't need much of an excuse to dole out a flogging.

She *had* to get out of there for good.

"*Where is she?*" Velina said, her high voice coming out in a strained whisper. The late summer sun had set an hour ago, and true night would be closing in fast. But a night spent in the cold moonlight of the Darkwood would be better than her smelly cot in the workhouse. She had bathed in a stream after leaving Drěghold that morning, eager to begin her new life. And now...

She clutched her bare arms, her straight silver hair doing little to warm her shoulders as it fell over them. Clouds shifted above, revealing a bulbous moon, and she raised her chin. One more try. She *had* to find the witch.

After taking one last look at the scrap of paper, she shoved it back into her pocket and set off again, ignoring the brambles in her hair and droplets of blood on her bare calves. Her dirty tunic only fell to her knees, offering little protection from the perils of the wood. She trudged back over the dry riverbed, scrambling up the stones on the steep bank. Her chest pounding with nervous energy, she rounded the hill rumored to be faerŭn and scrambled through the brambles again. Blood trickled down her legs from more scrapes, and here was the rock...

And a cottage. It stood in the shadow of the trees, past the rock shaped like a skull. Velina fell to her knees, her hand reaching for the rock. Hadn't she been standing here moments ago? She glanced between the cottage and the rock. The two shadowed holes on the rock seemed to meet her gaze. She bolted to her feet and strode toward the cottage, a chill running down the back of her neck. She shook herself. She must have gotten turned around or something, or didn't notice it in the deep shadows of the trees at the edge of the wood.

Vines trailed over the cottage roof and up the chimney, curling into the air like wisps of smoke with nothing to grasp. The building was made of weathered wood, a dilapidated porch covering the front and moss on the roof tiles. The front door was crooked, hanging by one hinge. And not a single light shone against the growing darkness.

Velina's steps slowed as she neared the place. She licked her lips, which were suddenly dry. Heart thundering in her ribcage, she stepped up onto the front porch, which let out a creak like a dying owl's screech. Her shoulders crept up to her ears. If anyone was inside, they now knew for certain that Velina was here.

There was no going back.

She swallowed, reaching her shaking hand toward the door. It was ancient and made from thick wood, its original color indiscernible, with cracks and crevices of age lining its surface. She paused. What would she bargain with the witch for? She had barely thought about her request. *Escape from her miserable life in Drëghold* wasn't enough. Her life had been just as miserable in Ravenshold. She was miserable everywhere—she'd been treated miserably ever since she was born. She pulled her hand away from the door, angrily throwing her silver hair back over her shoulder. She'd had silver hair since birth; it marked her as touched by the cursed faerŭn.

Whether the faerŭn really existed and swapped human babies with their own sick offspring, Velina didn't know. But everywhere she went, she was shunned as such and had to settle for the gods-forsaken workhouses to keep herself from starving to death. It had been so ever since she could remember, in all her nineteen or twenty years—she didn't actually know her age. Whoever named her had left her on the doorstep of an orphanage in Ravenshold, which, conveniently for everyone but her, had been adjacent to the workhouse. She'd grown up at the mercy of those larger and meaner than her, only good for her nimble fingers and ability to slip into narrow places—like behind a broken millwheel, where she ran the risk of getting caught in the wheel the moment she got the thing unstuck.

But last week, she'd vowed to leave the workhouse for good. Eghrŭn had flogged her in front of everyone for breaking his prized piece of milling equipment, which he'd just gotten from Ravenshold. Velina had been tasked with maintaining the machine since she could reach into its various nooks and crannies to make sure all the belts and gears were clean. Eghrŭn was about to sign a contract with some noble for a staggering sum of money and sent Velina to make sure the thing was pristine before showing it off to the noble. But she had mistaken an innocuous-looking bottle of vïloil for leather oil, and it had eaten away at the machine's belts. The accident had lost Eghrŭn a fortune, according to his angry snarls as the switch met her back in the workhouse courtyard. She couldn't go back there.

Her heart suddenly racing, Velina reached out and knocked on the witch's door, a jolt running through her stomach as soon as her knuckles touched the wood. A new life. One of her choosing. That was all she wanted.

"Hello?" she asked in her high, clear voice. "I'm looking for the witch."

The door swung open on its one hinge, a sad creaking just as miserable as the interior condition of the cottage. Moonlight slanted in through the open door. Dust smothered the one-room cottage, including the attic loft above the kitchen nook. Heavy shadows leered at her from the hearth, which was cold and black. Cupboard doors hung open to reveal barren insides. And there wasn't a soul in sight.

Velina swayed and clutched the doorframe, pressing her eyes closed for a moment. The wood felt solid under her fingertips. Sturdy. Like the cottage would stand for eons after everyone in Viridia was long dead. Steadying herself on the threshold, she lurched inside, gritting her teeth. The smell wasn't as bad as she'd expected; an earthy, almost herbal scent stole over her. Bundles of herbs hung over the hearth, long since dried and coated in dust, but a pleasant sight to look at, nonetheless.

A lengthy sigh escaped from deep inside her chest,

and she shifted the door closed behind her, propping it up with its one rusty hinge, which further deepened the shadows of the cottage. The grimy windows let in a cool glow of moonlight, allowing her to see only the outlines of the interior. Disappointment weighed heavy in her chest, but what she needed most was somewhere to sit and rest.

She spotted an old rocking chair by the hearth and dragged herself over to it, exhaustion suddenly pressing on her bones. At least she was out of Drěghold. And she had a roof over her head for the night. In the morning, she could do some foraging for something to eat.

Velina couldn't stay here indefinitely. The cottage wasn't far enough from Drěghold, but perhaps it was enough for now.

espite everything, Velina wasn't sleepy, so she rose from the old rocking chair and explored the cottage in the dim moonlight filtering in through the dirty windows. Upon her first inspection, she located a small stack of firewood tucked next to the hearth and flint left carelessly on the mantle. She made quick work of them and soon stood before a modest fire. Warmth radiated from the hearth, and she gazed into the merrily crackling flames. Her belly growled in hunger, but she was used to that. Going to sleep was usually her remedy. She could better assess the cottage in the daylight anyway.

Too afraid to climb up into the dark loft—she'd been struck with the sudden realization that the witch who lived here definitely didn't live here anymore and could be *dead* here—she curled up in the old rocking chair with a tattered shawl draped around her shoulders.

She shivered, shrugging off the terrible thoughts. *If there was a dead witch up there*, she reasoned, *the cottage wouldn't smell so nice.* The ancient-looking flowers and herbs hanging from the mantle even seemed to have some life left in them. But still, Velina couldn't stop the intrusive images of the loft from invading her mind. The sudden thought that the shawl might have belonged to the witch made her sit up straight and look around the dark cottage, as if her thoughts might summon the witch—or her ghost. But no, she reasoned, surely a passing traveler had left it. And she didn't have anything else to keep her warm. She wriggled in the chair, forcibly closing her eyes. Tomorrow, she'd go out and look for food, and everything would be better. Wishing for abundance in the forest outside, she sighed and turned her head to a more comfortable position.

Before she could doze off into a proper sleep, she heard footsteps creak on the porch. She shot like a bolt out of the chair. Her heart raced as she stood frozen, but with the fire crackling in the hearth, and the sound of the chair rocking back and forth, whoever stood on the porch must know there was someone inside.

Was it the witch? Would she lay a curse on Velina for intruding? Or had someone come nosing around, looking for a runaway faerŭn girl from the workhouse?

The person stood silent for a moment, as if undergoing the same hesitation Velina had felt earlier, then finally knocked. "I'm looking for the witch," the person said, making it sound more like a question than a statement.

Velina clutched the shawl about her as her gaze darted around the cottage. She couldn't hide. They knew she was in here. But they were looking for the witch.

"Please," the voice said. "I can pay."

Heart hammering, she stared at the poorly secured door, wishing she could see through its planks to determine the intentions of the stranger. She yanked the shawl up over her hair and noticeably pointy ears, draping it around herself like the Mosu nuns in Ravenshold did. She could pretend to be the witch, take their money, and be long gone by morning. She took two steps toward the door and paused, instantly regretting the movement. What if this was some sort of trick or a trap?

What if it was the witch?

She swallowed a hard lump in her throat. Her aching belly was no better for it. She was about to change her mind and find a dark corner to hide in when she heard a heavy sigh outside, the kind she recognized. It was a sigh of defeat. Of desperation.

Before she could change her rattled mind once more, she lowered her voice and said, "Coming." Re-checking the shawl, she hunched in on herself, then opened the door a sliver. "What is it?" Velina growled, doing her best to remain in the shadows. The clear skies painted a dark picture for her, highlighted in moonlight.

Another sigh came from the boy who faced her. She pulled back a little as he tried to peer inside. He looked about her age from what little she could see of his hooded visage; he was about her height and wore dark clothing of a high quality if the neat stitching and stiff fabrics were any indication. He tucked a pair of leather riding gloves into an interior pocket of his cloak, and she caught a flash of a pocket watch chain. "Thank the Omens," he said. "I've been searching all night. Went three times around the wood, in fact—"

A snort ripped from her, having done the same exact thing. She pinned him with a look as if it were a ruse she herself had planned for him. "And?" she asked.

"And...I've come seeking your help. I have coin. I—"

Velina made as if to close the door. "Explain or go away," she said, beginning to like this role of annoyed witch. It *was* late, and she *did* want him to go away.

He cleared his throat, and said, "Apologies, I..." He collected his words. "I need a spell, or whatever it is you do—to stop a marriage."

"A marriage?" she asked dryly. "And why would I do that? Trying to ruin someone's life, are you?"

"It's my own life, thank you very much," he retorted. "I mean—that's to say, I'm the one supposed to get married, and I'd like it stopped."

Velina withdrew farther behind the door. What was this stranger up to? "And what is the reasoning behind this...need?" she asked out of genuine curiosity.

He bristled. "I don't think you need to know—"

"I need to know intentions," she snapped, heat searing her cheeks, "if I am to find the correct way to...aid you." She held her breath, angry at herself for letting her curiosity steer this cursed conversation.

What was she even doing?

"Well...I..." He huffed. He looked for a second as if he would leave, taking whatever coin he had in his pockets with him. Perhaps she was being too harsh. She wanted him to go away, true, but the idea of having some coin to give her a life outside of the workhouses was too inviting.

She sniffed. "You must give me more information when you return tomorrow night," she said finally.

"Tomorrow?"

"Yes," Velina said slowly. "You will pay me a small sum now, so I may begin my ministrations. And tomorrow, you must return with..." She wracked her brain. What would a witch require for a spell such as this? Her stomach growled. "The thigh bone of a goose."

"The..." he began. An owl chose that moment to sing its eerie hooting song amid the moonlit trees, causing him to twitch. She gave him what she hoped was a mysterious look. "Yes, yes, of course," he said. He reached into a pocket and withdrew a coin pouch, emptying about half into his palm. He held it out to her.

Easing the door open enough to slip her hand out, she prayed her work-worn hands would pass as an old witch's. *Though, who was to say the witch had been old?* She snatched the coins out of his hand, the unfamiliar cold weight in her hand warming to her skin.

"Wait—" he cried. "When am I to return?"

"The same time tomorrow. And don't forget—"

"The thigh bone," he said, nodding, "of a goose. I won't. And you promise, you can help?"

"Indeed," she managed, not feeling the least bit bad about it. Sure, she could help him out of his coins—he looked like he could spare what was in his coin purse and twenty times more, from what she'd seen of his clothing and soft hands.

She slammed the door before he could see through her ruse, and she froze there, waiting for him to go away.

When his steps finally retreated over the creaky porch boards, she slumped back against the door. She squeezed the unforgiving coins in her palm, her stomach hollow, as she stared up at the darkness of the loft.

She thought it would take ages to fall asleep in the witch's cottage, alone, and in fear of another supplicant or even the witch herself barging in. But not long after curling up in the rocking chair, using the shawl as a blanket, her tired eyelids closed off the world. Guilt over taking the boy's money began to outweigh the hollow pit of hunger in her stomach.

The morning found her pacing the cottage, her thoughts at war with each other. Her first instinct—upon waking with aching bones in the rocking chair—was to run. Get as far from Drĕghold and Eghrŭn as possible. She had the boy's coins, more than she'd ever possessed in her life. But tonight, he would bring more. And what if she dragged this out even longer?

She could amass a large enough sum to afford a real place to live, perhaps even in Elody. Many a traveling merchant spoke reverently of the place, where one could retire to a quiet life among the salty breezes off the seashore. She could work on a fisherman's boat— perhaps buy her own if she could get enough money off this noble. Then she would never have to step foot in another workhouse again.

In the daylight, she inspected the cottage a little more as she paced. The ground floor held little besides the rocking chair and an old wooden table she hardly trusted upon seeing how some of the legs were leaning. A more reliable-looking ladder led up to the small loft, but she wasn't ready to inspect up there just yet—even the daylight hadn't chased away her fears from last night. The windows were grimy, but they let in a pleasant, green-tinged light from the trees shading the cottage. Dust had gathered on the windowsills and in every nook and cranny she saw. The hearth was serviceable, with a thick wooden beam for a mantle hung with old herbs and smooth round stones leading the chimney up the cottage wall.

Her belly growled, and she stopped pacing. The dusty kitchen nook under the loft held a work-worn wooden counter and half a dozen empty cabinets, but she had no food to fill them. Her hand went to the ill-gotten coins in her pocket. There was no way she could go back to Drĕghold for food, though. Eghrŭn and his minions roamed the streets daily, looking for urchins to "take in" for the workhouse. They would spot her in an instant.

The forest might have berries to forage, and she knew how to prepare meat, if she could get her hands on any. *If only I had a weapon...* With renewed interest, she looked around the cottage for anything she could use to gather food.

After turning about only once, she found a bow and full quiver propped up behind the door. She dashed over and inspected the string on the bow, running her fingers up and down it. She plucked it, her stomach leaping at her good fortune. Perhaps a traveling hunter had forgotten it here recently after taking shelter in the abandoned cottage. Not for the first time, she wondered what had happened to the real witch.

She seized the bow and strapped the quiver to her back. The underforeman in the Drĕghold workhouse had let some of the workers hunt in the surrounding woods under strict supervision a few years ago, if only to offset the costs of feeding them during that lean winter. He put an end to it though, after discovering the fresh air and freedom from the grimy machines inside the workhouse gave the workers too much joy.

Velina herself had never used a bow, but she'd seen enough from their brief excursions to know which end of the arrow to point. She had always gotten stuck collecting roots and nuts alone; even the other workers wanted nothing to do with a faerŭn girl.

"Now, if only I had a..." She glanced about the room again. "Basket," she said in surprise—for there was one sitting on the counter in the kitchen nook. She ran over to grab the thing, then tossed the shawl over her head. She didn't need anyone reporting to Eghrŭn that they'd seen a silver-haired girl in the Darkwood.

Basket hung from her belted skirt, she set out into the woods. The boy wouldn't be back until well after sundown, so she had all day to forage. The woods looked far more cheerful than usual, but she knew it must be the coin in her pocket, and the promise of a new life just at her fingertips. The idea of settling in Elody hovered in the back of her mind, and as she walked among the hard-bark trees of the woods, stalking what she thought was a hare, she made her plans.

Three nights. Three payments from the noble boy—and she already had one. Three times as much would buy her very own dwelling in the seaside town, far from the muddy streets of all the cities she'd ever lived in.

Her basket quickly filled up with the berries and nuts she came across, but also hefty clumps of bright-smelling dew weed and a bundle of lavender. She would need to make a more convincing witch if she wanted to keep this ruse up another two nights.

The hare she thought she was stalking turned out to be a very large and slow chipmunk, which she came nowhere near striking when she fired an arrow at it. A laugh bubbled from her throat when the creature got away, darting over an old stone wall. Her basket was full enough that it didn't matter. She'd found food aplenty, though her previous jaunts through the Darkwood had only ever produced a fraction of the harvest amid the brambles and barren scrub.

A moment of panic seized her when, after retracing her steps, she returned to the place where she thought the cottage should be and didn't find the skull rock. But there was the witch's cottage, the vines atop the chimney shrinking away from last night's fire. The way the sun shone on the worn wooden planks looked far more inviting than the cottage had looked last night in the near dark. Even the trees today looked more inviting. She chuckled at herself; perhaps her newfound freedom from the workhouse and having a temporary place to call home were making her see things differently. Relief washed through her, and she slung the basket higher up on her forearm.

As she had the previous night, Velina paused on the porch. What if the witch had returned while she was away? She shook her head and opened the door to find the cottage in the same state she'd left it in. It *was* a witch's cottage, after all. Who would dare trespass here? Well, apart from a desperate girl with the unfortunate fate of being born with silver hair.

Hardly taking the time to set her things down, she had a handful of berries in her mouth before she could think to ration them. The name of the berries escaped her—she'd never eaten the red fruits before, though she'd seen plenty of them on Eghrŭn's table. The hazelnuts and wild peas she'd found were just as heavenly. She quickly found the bottom of the basket. She hadn't eaten her fill in longer than she could remember. Had she ever eaten her fill?

At least she'd have plenty to eat from the forest for the next two days. Her stomach ached again, but this was a new sensation...too full? She chuckled at the new sensation and clutched her belly. She'd have to stock up for her trip to Elody. It would be at least a few days' walk.

Velina wished there was a way she could stay in the cottage. Really, it was perfect for her. Plenty to forage, a warm fire, a space to call her own—it was more than she'd had in her entire life. It was all she really wanted. But it was far too close to Drĕghold, less than half a day's walk. She longed to put leagues between herself and that workhouse, and worst of all, Eghrŭn.

She drew in a breath and looked around the cottage again. She should start preparing for her meeting with the boy tonight. She had hours yet, but the cottage still looked dilapidated and un-lived in. If she were to convince him to come back yet another night for the services of "the witch," she would have to put on a better act. First, she needed to clean.

Velina found a broom in the corner of the kitchen area and got to work batting down cobwebs. Tying the shawl over her mouth and nose, she kicked up what seemed like decades of dirt. How long had it been since the real witch had inhabited this place?

She threw open the door, intent on banishing the immense pile of dirt she'd collected, when she saw something that made her leap back, wielding the broom like a weapon.

A scrawny gray cat perched on the edge of the porch.

Her heart pounding like a blacksmith's iron, she yanked down the shawl from her face and exclaimed, "You scared me!"

The cat *meowed* moodily and tried to push its way past her into the cottage.

"Oy, get back," she chastised it, blocking it with the broom.

It gave her a baleful look, as if to say, *If you can trespass here, why can't I?* She huffed, maintaining her hold on the broom. The workhouse back in Drěghold had cats aplenty. A particularly mean gray striped one often stole the few bread heels she hoarded in her cot. Not to mention the felines did their rat hunting jobs *too* efficiently to allow her and the other workers any hope of extra meat.

"I don't have any food for you," Velina told the cat.

Just then, a scratching sound above Velina's head caused her attention to shift upward to the porch rafters. She knew that sound, and so did the cat.

"Great. Mice," Velina muttered. Then she pinned the cat with a look. "Fine, but you're on your own. I've got things to do, and I'll be gone soon." She shifted the broom, and the cat darted inside like a predator on the hunt. Velina resumed the forced exodus of dirt. Soon a cloud of dust hung in the air like a filthy ghost lingering on the porch.

Back inside, her gaze flitted up to the loft above the kitchen nook, where the cat now perched. Velina's stomach clenched. Thoughts of dead witches in the loft intruded, and she shot an inquisitive look at the cat.

"Anybody up there?" Velina asked quietly. The cat *meowed* uninterestedly and rolled onto its side, tail lolling off the edge of the loft. Taking that for as much reassurance as the cat would give her, she hitched the shawl back over her mouth and nose, and mounted the ladder, broom in hand. As she crested the edge of the loft floor, her gut clenched something hideous, her wild eyes took in the musty scene. Relief washed over her body like a warm spring rain. There was nothing but an old blanket folded in the corner, and a small open crate with some dusty bottles and books.

With a sigh, she glanced at the cat and offered him a reluctant smile. *If only there was more light up here, it would be such a nice space. A window or something.* She got to work sweeping. The cat occasionally shifted out of the broom's way, but he seemed to prefer the high perch.

As she poked about the back of the loft, her sleeve caught on a rogue nail sticking out of the wall, and she jerked back lest she tear her only tunic. As she disentangled herself, she noticed the board behind the nail was loose. There was light coming from behind it; not only light—glass.

After a few minutes of prying, trying to insert the broom handle, and muttering curses, she unearthed a window that had been boarded up. The glass was clouded with age like the rest of the cottage windows, so she couldn't make out the woods outside, but it offered as much light as she needed.

"Omens," she said in awe. The light revealed how much more cleaning she had to do, but also designs painted on the ceiling—swirling strokes of mint green and purple as deep as wine and what looked like a few runes woven in between the swirls. Now *this* looked the way a witch's cottage should look.

After the loft was clear of dirt, she had to redouble her efforts on the main floor, as a fresh coat had settled on all the surfaces. It must have been hours past midday when she finally wiped the gritty sweat from her brow and surveyed her work.

The fresh lavender and dew weed hung from the mantle, and she'd tossed the old herbs into the ashes in the hearth, where they'd smoldered like weak incense. The kitchen had been scrubbed with the help of a bucket she'd found on the porch and filled with water from a nearby stream. The cottage was beginning to look rather respectable. She felt another pang of sadness at the knowledge she couldn't stay.

She was slinging her basket over her forearm to go forage again when she heard steps on the porch. She thanked the Omens she'd closed the door earlier to prevent the cloud of dust from returning inside. Heat flooded to her chest. She had come to accept that the witch was long gone, but it didn't escape her that by now, Eghrŭn must have surely noticed a certain faerŭn-touched girl was missing. She set down the foraging basket and tried to slow her breathing, almost tripping on the wash bucket on her way to grab the shawl, which she'd set to air on the back of the rocking chair.

"Hello?" a voice called from the porch, accompanied by a timid knock. She froze. It was the boy from last night.

"A moment," she growled, yanking the shawl over

her hair and making sure it covered every silver strand. He was early, and it was still light out!

The cat was dozing on the edge of the loft, having caught a mouse or two during her cleaning session. Velina noticed the tip of the cat's tail was black, like it had been dipped in ink. She gave the creature half a smile. *After all, every witch needs a cat.*

Giving the cottage a once-over glance and finding it passable even in daylight, she wrenched open the off-kilter door a few inches.

"What is it?" she demanded.

He started, dropping the velvet pouch he'd been fumbling with. He bent down to get it and looked up into her face. "Oh! I—I'm sorry—I..." His gaze settled on her face, and her cheeks started to burn. Now that she could see him in the dimming afternoon light, she was sure he was about her age and possessed alarmingly golden eyes and raven black hair.

"You're early," she said.

"It—it's you? The witch I met last night?"

"Of course it is," she said, crossing her arms over her chest.

He looked at the shawl and nodded. "My apologies. I thought you were much—" He stared in disbelief at her face.

Curses, she thought. *He must have thought me some wizened old witch, and now...* "You thought what I wanted you to think," she blurted out enigmatically.

His throat bobbed as he swallowed, nervous.

Good. "But again: You're early. I haven't had time

to finish preparing..." What? She hadn't prepared anything that might look like a spell to grant his wish. She'd been too focused on cleaning and making the cottage look like a witch lived here.

Her stomach growled, and her gaze darted to the empty basket on the table. What was she supposed to do? The boy needed a wish granted—to get him out of a marriage, apparently. When *she* had come here seeking the witch's help, she'd pictured the witch brewing a potion or something. *If only the cottage had some kind of cauldron, or...*

The bottom dropped out of her stomach. There, on a hook over the fireplace, hung a heavy black cauldron, which had *definitely* not been there before.

She gathered her wits, slowly. She needed this noble's money...whether or not the cottage had started making things appear at her very thought. She suppressed a hysterical giggle.

Omens, she thought, a swirl of excitement brewing in her chest. *The broom, the bow, the basket.* She'd inspected the cottage last night. And thinking about it, she realized none of those things had been here. The *cottage* was magic.

"I'm sorry," the boy said. "Is something wrong?"

"No, no," she blurted out, her mind reeling. "You're early is all. I need time." Time to make it look like she was brewing a potion for him anyway. But the cottage had provided. *I wish I had more ingredients,* she thought to herself.

He bowed his head, muttering, "I know. I'm sorry."

Out of the corner of her eye, she saw that the formerly barren kitchen shelves now housed a new collection of bottles filled with herbs and who knew what else—each a different shape or color and each marked with a neat label. Her heart leapt. The cottage really was magic. And after all her cleaning efforts, the kitchen looked cozier than ever with the jars and bottles taking up space on the wooden shelves.

The boy went on, seemingly oblivious, as Velina's heart soared. "But I brought the goose bone, and I—I really need this. My father received word from my intended's family this morning. It's moving a lot quicker than I expected."

She narrowed her eyes at him, brought back to her current predicament, though her mind was awash in the possibilities of what the cottage could do. How had she not even noticed? She thought back to when she was cleaning the loft, and how she wanted a window when the nail snagged her...

"And I—er—brought you a gift," he said, more brightly. Without waiting for a reply, he began digging in a satchel and withdrew a glass jar of slow-moving amber liquid. "It's from my own personal hives."

Her mouth popped open at the sight of the honey. How well-off he must be to keep his own bees! Her insides staggered between feeling bad about tricking him out of his money and realizing how easily he could afford it and more. She was beginning to feel like the wicked witch she was pretending to be.

She clenched her stomach. "Very well." He handed her the honey, and as she withdrew to find somewhere to put it down, he followed her inside, apparently taking that as an invitation. *Omens!*

But she hadn't spent the morning cleaning the

cottage for nothing. She scoffed quietly at herself. *If only I'd asked the cottage to help me clean.*

With the boy directly behind her, she thought swiftly, *I wish it looked more like I actually lived here,* hoping it wasn't too vague of an instruction. She hoped the boy would leave soon so she could experiment with the magic more.

Slinking back toward the fireplace where the cauldron now hung, Velina took in the cottage at the same time he did...because she was seeing much of it for the first time too.

A new rug sat under the table, which now stood on four sturdy legs of gleaming dark wood, with a vase of wildflowers atop it. The kitchen had cleaned itself up better, with even more little bottles and jars lined up neatly at the back of the counter. A garland of flowers hung across the rafters leading to the loft, and a pot of tea sat brewing by the kitchen window. Just for something to do, she strode over and poured a cup in an elated daze.

She gulped down her first sip of the too-hot tea, then adjusted her scarf. *Right,* she thought rationally. *Even if it's a magical cottage, I still can't stay here. Eghrŭn will likely find out I was looking for the witch. The traveling tinker is still in Drĕghold, and some of the others must have seen me talking to him.* Eghrŭn could be the next person knocking on her door. She needed the money, and she needed to leave soon, even though the promise of this place nearly broke her heart.

She took another sip of the tea, which had

thankfully cooled down a little. She didn't think it would be very witch-like of her to offer the boy any, so instead she strode over to the cauldron to inspect it. The noble boy was still standing near the door, looking nervously up at the cat, which was cleaning itself. He tripped on his own feet as he turned away from the cat, then clasped his hands behind his back as if to cover up his clumsiness.

To her delight, the cauldron was already filled with water. She adjusted her scarf again, ensuring her silver hair was covered. On instinct, she grabbed the bundle of dew weed and pulled off a sprig, taking great care to look mysteriously intentional about everything she was doing. Crumbling the dew weed into the simmering water, she glanced at him over her shoulder and said, "I will begin the potion now; I was planning on foraging for more blackfork leaf this afternoon, but I...might have enough. I got the rest of the ingredients this morning. What is the name of your intended? I need more information for the spell."

At her final word, his shoulders crept up by his ears. She was thoroughly impressed with her monologue, and he seemed to be too. By the Omens, she just had to be convincing enough to come back with that third payment tomorrow. Unless the cottage could provide...

As he awkwardly cleared his throat, she thought to herself, *I wish I had more money.* She had already sequestered the first coins the boy had given her in her threadbare pocket, which was looped around her waist under her skirt. She slipped her hand through the slit in her skirt but found no additional coins. Glancing around the cottage revealed no mysterious sums of money either. There must be limits to the cottage's powers. Of course money would be one of them.

"Well?" she demanded, meeting his gaze.

"I—er—*my father's going to kill me*," he muttered. He broke off eye contact and gazed at the floor instead, then spoke louder. "You won't tell anyone about this?"

"I swear it," she said. What did she care about the goings-on of nobles?

He let out a steadying breath, and said, "Lady Morina de Wrestia."

"Wrestia?" she demanded. "But isn't the lady quite..." She looked him up and down. He couldn't be more than a year older than her. And the lady she'd seen parading through Drĕghold once had been white of hair and wrinkled of face. She remembered the day quite well. Eghrŭn had withheld dinner that night for anyone who had been caught outside the workhouse to watch the stately procession.

"Oh, no," he blustered. "You must be thinking of her mother. Morina the Younger is the lady to whom I am promised."

"Hmm," Velina said. "Well, at least you're getting the younger." She sauntered over to the potion bottles on the wall by the kitchen and made a show of selecting a few jars. She was almost enjoying the witch persona now.

"Age isn't the problem," the boy offered reluctantly.

She opened the jar of blackfork leaves and was about to reach her hand in when she saw how sharp they were. She'd only ever heard descriptions of them. A ridge of black slivers ran down each edge of the leaves. *I wish I had something to get these leaves out of the jar.* A pair of tweezers appeared on the mantle. Her heart soared. She hadn't even meant to ask the cottage. *Thank you,* she added in her thoughts.

She seized the tweezers, delicately plucking out three of the spiky black leaves one at a time and dropping them into the cauldron. The water sizzled each time a leaf touched it, drawing a satisfied smirk out of Velina. How conveniently magical.

The boy had lapsed into melancholy, no doubt stewing over his predicament, so she asked, "And what is your name?"

He eyed the honey jar on the table as if it were his only friend in the room and could lend him a hand navigating the conversation. The jar did him no such favors, however, so he reluctantly offered, "Will."

"Will what? I need it for the spell." And by the Omens, she was burning with curiosity by now. Who would not want to wed the most eligible noble daughter in the northern country of Wrestia? The stories she'd heard from the tinkers alone painted the palace in silver and marble, second to no other monument except perhaps their famed ice gardens.

"Ravenson," he whispered.

"Ravenson?" she demanded in shock. "And you traveled all this way?" When the workhouse in

Ravenshold had practically sold her to Eghrŭn, she'd taken a two-day ride via farm cart to Drĕghold. How had he gone home and back so quickly? Perhaps he was staying in Drĕghold.

He shrugged, saying defensively, "I can ride. It's not that far."

"Oh," she said, her face flaming. Of course he had a horse, which would be much faster than a cart. Even still, it was not a short distance between the two holdings. He must really be desperate. *I wish I could help him for real.* But she had a feeling the cottage's magic wouldn't extend as far as Wrestia, and unless the cauldron turned her random selection of herbs into an actual magic potion, she was of no use to him. She was more likely to poison him, with how little knowledge of herbcraft she possessed. She wished for a sufficiently-witchy looking spoon, and was rewarded with a gnarled old wooden spoon hanging from a nail on the mantle. She smiled sadly at it as she lifted it.

"They're leaving tomorrow afternoon," he blurted out as she stirred the mixture carefully. "I need to stop this wedding."

Guilt seizing her chest, she bowed her head as she continued stirring. The first payment he'd given her wasn't enough. She needed more if she were to set out on her own. "I understand," she said quietly. "But this particular potion takes twenty hours to brew. And did you bring the ingredient I asked for?"

Maybe after he left, she could think of something to ask the cottage for—something that would *actually* help him. Her stomach was turning as sour as her black potion looked.

"Yes, of course," Will said, pulling the velvet bag he'd dropped earlier from his satchel. He extended it toward her, and she stepped back.

"You need to put it into the cauldron yourself and think of your desire as you do so," she explained morosely, having just come up with the idea. Perhaps the cottage would hear his plea and help him.

As the goose bone entered the liquid, a black sheen on the surface of the potion retracted to the edges, earning a gasp from Will. She was a horrible fraud. But the Ravensons—the ruling nobles of Ravenshold— could afford to lose a few hundred gold to a runaway posing as a witch.

She swallowed. "There is much more work to be done to the potion, and it must brew for twenty hours. I will take payment now, and again when you return tomorrow."

He balked. "But I was hoping..." He sighed, the forlorn exhale drawing pain into her own lungs. He brushed a hand through his black hair and nodded, then withdrew a pouch from inside his vest.

She crept over to him, at war with herself, and held out her hand. But he was looking up at her hair.

Her hair.

"Y-you're—"

Her insides froze, and she lifted her chin. Her shawl had slipped. "What did you expect?" she managed in a whisper, moving her hands slowly to fix the shawl, while trying to hide how badly she was shaking. She had gone and foiled the whole thing. Omens-cursed, stupid faerŭn.

Will swallowed. He didn't stop staring at her, even though she'd covered up the silver hair and subtly pointed ears. She waited for him to recoil, or yell, or demand his coin back. At the very least, she expected him to storm away muttering prayers to the Omens. But he just stood there.

"Well?" she finally demanded, unable to take it any longer.

"Nothing," Will said. "I'll be back tomorrow. I—I really need this to work, Mistress Witch. When can I return?"

Now it was her turn to gape in silence. That was all? After the treatment she'd always been given for her Omens-cursed hair and ears? He must really be desperate. *Or perhaps, the faerŭn aren't any more feared than witches*, she thought.

Well, she could be both. She put a hand on her chin, thinking. "You...may return an hour's strike after sunrise—*and no earlier*. I suppose I can hurry some of the other steps this evening. That is, if you leave soon." She longed to test the magic of the cottage, and his presence only filled her with immense guilt.

Will bobbed his head. "Of course, of course. I'll be back in the morning." He headed for the door without further word.

"Are you staying in Drĕghold?" she asked his retreating back. It would be bad for a noble to be seen entering and exiting Drěghold this often. Especially if he was known to be looking for the witch. That would draw attention she really didn't need.

He turned, his dark eyebrows furrowed. "No, Mistress. Ravenshold."

"Safe journey then," she said, still muddled. He'd barely get back to Ravenshold and have to turn back around for the morning. She shook her head and watched him go. What did she know about how long it took on horseback?

With her back to the closed door, she heard the muffled snorting of a horse, then hooves retreating at a trot through the woods. *I wish I had something stronger than tea to drink*, she thought, and a dark amber bottle appeared on the table beside the honey. She sighed, her chest heaving.

She was just as wicked as a witch.

Shadows wreathed the windows as Velina hunched over the cauldron. She had emptied it of the noxious concoction shortly after Will left, the bitter blackfork fumes getting to her, then cleaned and filled it with a foraged stew of sorts—potatoes and a hapless chicken she'd found wandering outside. But she'd already exhausted her mental list of ways to actually help Will.

Asking the cottage to make a magical potion was not an option. She'd tested that one by asking for a magic potion to turn her hair as yellow as cornsilk, and nothing had appeared.

I wish I had a map of the continent, Velina thought. When she turned to look at the table, an open scroll covered the surface. Her fingertips pored over the ink. She couldn't read any of the words, but handy illustrations accompanied many of the cities, and she quickly identified Ravenshold and Drĕghold by their crests. The distance *was* great, she wasn't imagining it. How in the name of the Omens Will was able to ride there and back confounded her to no end.

Her finger landed on Elody. Oh, the tales she'd heard from passing tinkers! Of white sands and ships filled with merry traders come to port. Of salty breezes and the blazing sun. No muddy streets, dank belowground sleeping rooms, or cities full of dour faces.

She stalked about the cottage, muttering wishes. Some of them came true, like the comfortable pair of shoes she absently wished for after stubbing her toe on the rocking chair. Then she distracted herself by asking for various items of clothing, which she found fit her perfectly. Next, she asked for a large knapsack, to carry as much food and whatever items she could ask the cottage for. She wished for an extra of each article of clothing, a waterskin, a dagger for hunting, and a wide-brimmed hat. Several oilcloths for wrapping up the food she would forage.

"I should just leave tonight," she muttered, packing everything neatly into the sack for a second time. She bit her lip. She had most of the money. Perhaps she didn't need the third payment after all—particularly now that she had all these clothes and belongings.

She groaned. "How can I help him?" she demanded. The cat raised its head from its loft perch and gave her a scornful eye. She rolled her eyes. "He doesn't want to marry Lady Morina for some reason. He's a perfectly eligible noble. Perhaps he doesn't like the cold?" The feline merely stretched and turned away, ignoring her.

I wish I had a black and...sparkly liquid in a jar that

is harmless to drink, she thought, her stomach wrenching. A glass jar with a fat round bottom and a narrow opening at the top sat on the table. A black and silver liquid swirled inside.

She put her hands on her cheeks. Was she really going to do this? Deceiving that poor boy who was kind enough to bring a *witch* his own honey? Shutting her eyes briefly, and then blinking away the sudden moisture, she shook her head. She still had time to come up with something else.

Though the loft was now clean, she wanted to sleep by the fire, so she wished for a few clean blankets, and let the cat keep his private perch in the loft. After balling up an extra blanket to put under her head—a luxury she'd never had before—she stared into the depths of the cottage ceiling trying to think of a way to help until she faded into oblivion.

No solutions magically appeared in her brain overnight, nor did they arrive in the morning as she made a positively delightful cup of tea with the cottage-provided tea leaves and Will's honey. She sat drinking the brew for a luxurious half hour.

Her stomach writhed at the thought of Will's impending visit. She had only the one solution—the hateful "potion" on the table—though perhaps she still had a little time to think of another. Even if he could afford being duped out of his coin, he seemed genuinely distraught about the whole marriage situation. No one should have to live a life they didn't want to lead.

She sighed and quickly finished off the dregs of her

tea. She really should get going. She had planned on foraging in the Darkwood before Will's visit and would need to keep an eye out for anyone from Drĕghold. Looping the basket over her forearm, she headed to the door for one last forage in the Darkwood. But when she stepped outside, the forest was dark and murky, and she quickly found herself being scraped by brambles. Gone were the bushes of green peas she'd picked from only yesterday. And the berries were nowhere to be seen. She stumbled along a dry riverbank, searching for the stone wall she'd chased the chipmunk down only yesterday.

A twig snapped behind her, causing her to freeze. A roar followed, and she spun around, feeling as if her neck had snapped from the force of it. She would know that orcish roar anywhere.

The towering form of Eghrŭn emerged from the trees and spilled out into the empty riverbed, the orc's green muscles heaving. Holding his heavy staff in one hand, he charged at her. "You little rat!" he snarled through his fangs. "How dare you run away!" His sparse black hair was ragged, and dark circles hung under his wide eyes; he'd clearly been searching through the night.

She scurried back up the side of the riverbed toward the cottage, her heart thundering in her chest. Roots tripped her, and she fell, but she could tell the cottage was nearby, so she scrambled to her feet and kept running. The cottage would protect her—she hoped.

"There's a decade more on your indenture, you silver-haired rat!" Eghrŭn called through the

Darkwood. "And I'll add another if you don't stop running!" It felt as if a cage of snakes had been set loose in her stomach as she sprinted for the cottage, which she could now see through the trees, the skull rock just beyond it.

Out of breath, she rushed up the porch and through the door. She slammed her small frame against the back of the broken door to hold it closed. "Please hide me from Eghrŭn," she panted. "I don't want to go back to Drĕghold!" Over and over she wished it, until she slid down the door, clutching her knees. And still, she continued whispering the words. Tears streamed down her face, as she waited for Eghrŭn's staff to come crashing into the door.

Her frenzied mind drifted to Elody and its sandy shores and how she would give anything in the world to be there rather than here. Eventually her heartbeat calmed, and slowly, her breath came back. She wiped the cold sweat from her brow with a shaking hand. Was he gone? How could he have possibly missed seeing the cottage? She didn't leave the door for a long time, even though her slim body would do nothing to keep Eghrŭn from bursting in should he choose to.

Finally, when she saw the rays of dawn peering through the cloudy cottage windows, she swallowed and backed a step away from the door. Silently she wished for something she'd seen some of the handlers at the workhouse wield. A heavy mace appeared in one hand, half a dozen small spikes sticking out of it. That made her feel a little better.

The cat in the loft meowed lazily, causing Velina to let out a crazed chuckle. Had she imagined it all? Surely, he hadn't been far behind her. But why hadn't he approached the cottage? Starting to think it was all a dream—perhaps drinking tea from a magical cottage wasn't such a good idea after all—she carefully pried open the door a sliver, heart in her throat.

Bright light met her eyes, and she shaded them. *What in the Omens...*

She opened the door a little farther, and her mouth went dry. Expecting to see Eghrŭn hunting her through the murky Darkwood, her gaze was instead met with white sands under the shade of a strange palm-like tree.

A loud meow sounded from behind her, and she whirled to see the cat leap from halfway down the ladder, then softly pad over to her. He sniffed at the salty air now wafting in from the half-open door.

Velina swallowed. "Is this—" Her voice cracked in a ragged way. "Elody?"

The cat sauntered outside and hopped off the porch onto the sand, immediately flopping onto his back and rolling in the stuff. Velina eased a tentative foot out the door, when a shushing sound met her ears.

Water, as far as the eye could see. Gentle waves breathing in and out at the edge, lapping at the sands. "Elody," she breathed. Warm tears fled from her eyes, and her heart raised as if to meet them. She had made it. The cottage...

The cottage. Its door had opened to a fruitful forest, so unlike the Darkwood, when she had needed food, where Will had found her and appeared affronted when she mentioned how far of a ride it was for him from Ravenshold. Had she been outside Ravenshold this whole time?

Ravenshold…Will… Her chest constricted.

And so, though the salty air was so close and true heaven awaited her here in Elody, she pulled her foot back in and beckoned for the cat. She savored the sound of the waves and the soft breeze on her cheek as she waited for the cat to saunter in. When they were both back inside the cottage, she shut the door firmly and closed her eyes. *I wish I were in Will's forest, outside Ravenshold.*

After a steadying breath, she opened her eyes, and pulled the door open a slit. She was shocked to see Will himself striding past the cottage, horse in tow.

"Will!" she called.

He turned, and then looked twice at her, eyes bulging. "H-How? I've been looking for your cottage for ages! I thought I knew where it was, but…"

An uncustomary smile burst over her face, and she beckoned him closer. He hobbled his horse to let it graze on the sweetgrass and leapt for the porch. "Is it ready?" he asked, excitement blazing on his face. It was as if a stone dropped into her stomach—a cold, slimy stone. Surely, her joyful smile would have invited that kind of interpretation. *Omens*, she thought, her gaze going to the fake potion on the table.

But then an idea struck her. "Come in," she said, almost pulling him inside the cottage.

He glanced at the jar on the table, his throat bobbing noticeably. His raven hair was ruffled in a charming way, and he was dressed even finer than usual in a stiff black collared coat. His hands toyed nervously with the bottom of his charcoal-colored vest.

"I've been doing some thinking," she said. "And I don't think the potion is the way to fix it."

"Oh?" Will was staring at her hair, which she belatedly realized had lost its covering. The shawl must have fallen off when Eghrŭn chased her through the Darkwood. She was still trying to figure out how she'd been sitting outside Ravenshold this whole time, except when she'd stepped out of the cottage this morning. But then she recalled her thoughts just before opening the cottage door—she'd been thinking about the Darkwood.

"I have another idea," she offered. "Hold on." She went over to the door and shut it tightly. She hoped the magic would work with someone else here. *I wish we were in Elody.* She repeated it in her head a few times for good measure. Nerves buzzing through her, she reached out and opened the door again.

White light blazed into the cottage, the morning sun in Elody farther advanced than Ravenshold. She tore her gaze from the shore to see Will's reaction.

His jaw hung open, golden eyes wide in amazement. "H-how..." He turned to her. "You're amazing."

Her face flooded with heat, and she looked down at the floorboards. "No, I'm...not. Look, this will help you, right? You can go to Elody, and—"

"Why would I need to go to Elody? What about this potion? Won't it work?"

Velina said nothing as her insides crumbled,

embarrassment flaring up and turning her face red. She shook her head.

"But you…" he said, confusion furrowing his brows as he gestured to the sands of Elody outside the door. "You're magic!"

She shook her head again. "It's the cottage," she said in a hollow voice.

"No. No… You were going to…" Velina stared at him. He swallowed, then nodded sadly. And then his gaze settled on the full knapsack by the door, and he spoke quietly, voice cracking, "Take me back to Ravenshold."

"But… But why?" she demanded. "Why don't you want to marry Morina of Wrestia? Is she a wicked person?"

He snorted, turning away from her. "Look, I don't know who you are or what you know of me, but I don't want to get married right now. I don't want to go to Wrestia. And on top of everything else, I don't want to leave Ravenshold and…and my bees."

"Your bees?"

As if he didn't hear her, he continued, "I've been forced into everything my whole life—combat training, even though I have no desire to strike another person. Courting, even though I have no interest in the matter. Mathematics… You get the idea. But my bees are the one thing *I* chose. When I was eight, I found a book on beekeeping in my father's library. When I was nine, I took in my first hive.

"I know it sounds stupid. But it's all I have for *me*."

His voice cracked again, and he took a step closer to the door. "I don't care that you were lying about the potion. I just thought you might...help. Now bring me back to Ravenshold, please."

A breath puffed out of her. His bees couldn't survive in Wrestia, shrouded in snow year-round. It was so simple. "And she can't come live with you in Ravenshold?" she asked meekly.

He shook his head. "The contract is final, and she won't move out of Wrestia. The match was so advantageous, my parents didn't even inform me until it was nearly a done deal. The only thing that would stop it now is if she doesn't arrive in time for the wedding feast."

"Truly?" she managed, her nose wrinkling. Nobles were so strange and fickle in their customs.

"It has something to do with commitment and the cycle of the moons and money, of course." He waved his hand vaguely.

"I wasn't trying to run away," she blurted out. "I really did want to help you." Will lifted his shoulders in half a shrug, waiting. She swallowed the bile in her throat and shut the door tight. She hauled in a breath, and before she asked the cottage for his request, held the air tight in her lungs.

"What if there was another way?" she asked him. His golden eyes rose to hers as if hardly daring to believe anything she said. "You know, this cottage can go pretty much anywhere—I *think*."

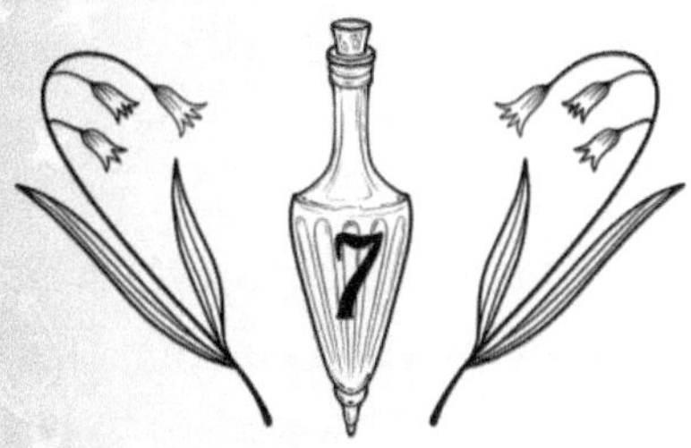

A bitter cold assailed Velina's face as she trudged through ankle-deep snow, swathed in thick furs. She had to yank her hood back over her head as the wind threw it back once more. The cottage did indeed go anywhere; at least, it went to Wrestia. And now, Velina completely understood why Will wouldn't want to live here, bees notwithstanding.

After peering out the crooked wooden door to ascertain the location, she had asked the cottage to supply her with a suitable outfit and a few other things. She had no time to waste if she wanted to delay the lady of Wrestia from her departure.

Guilt thick in her chest, she had told Will how to ask the cottage for what he needed. She lit a cozy fire and supplied him with a hot pot of tea before leaving. Still befuddled at seeing the snowscape after their brief jaunt to the sea, he nodded and retreated to sit beside the fire, clutching the cup like a life raft. Velina had then headed out into the snowstorm, leaving Will behind with the cat.

Halfway between the woods and the city, she belatedly wished she had asked the cottage for another underlayer and some warmer socks. Her toes had gone numb in the first ten minutes of trudging toward the city she could see in the rolling snowy hills. Her white fur cloak allowed her to pass through the icy gates with no trouble, as long as she kept her face down. The guards bowed to her, and she started walking slower.

She had reluctantly chosen to display her hair, asking the cottage for some white chalk and making quick work of rubbing the chalk down her silver strands to lighten them before donning her cloak. And so, with white hair and dressed as Morina the Elder, she strode through the streets of Wrestia and was stopped by no one. After all, she'd been pretending to be someone she wasn't for the past few days. She was getting the hang of it.

When she reached the palace, she shunned the regal front doors and strode purposefully around, looking for the place she needed. If Will was right, there was still time.

She found the stables and slipped inside, holding her head high. It wasn't long until she found what she needed. True to Will's expectation, the nobles of Wrestia were readying to depart for Ravenshold—immediately, she gathered from the teaming servants packing their carriages. If they missed the wedding feast, the marriage would be null. Nobles were so strange.

Velina reached into her deep coat pocket and

retrieved one of the glass vials she'd asked the cottage for. She stalked closer to the fanciest-looking carriage. It was laden with luggage, and the horses were already tethered to it. She could hear shouting not too far off—just inside the palace entrance from here. She didn't have much time.

The horses stamped their feet nervously when Velina came closer, and she patted the nearest flank. "Don't worry," she said. "You'll be fine."

Another shout rang out from the palace, something about one last trunk—and Velina yanked the cork off the first vial with extreme care.

She had learned her lesson about vïloil several days ago, and now she was putting it to good use. She dowsed every leather strap that connected the horses to the carriage, being careful not to get the vïloil on anything but the leather and bolts. Sure, it conditioned metal fantastically, but the leather would melt like snow on coal once any pressure was applied—this time, to her benefit.

She dashed around the first carriage and then the second, but before she was halfway through the second carriage—presumably the daughter's, based on the errant shouts about hatboxes—she heard footsteps in the stables.

A young page approached, face wrinkled in annoyance until he saw Velina and her chalk white hair. Then he froze, staring at her.

"L-Lady Morina?" he stuttered, glancing back at the palace from which he'd come.

Just then a shout came, clear as a bell. "Abson! My daughter needs the third hatbox after all. I will permit one more minute until we depart! We *cannot* be late, and she was already tardy from her morning pedicure!"

The page glanced from Velina back to the door in confusion. She cursed the Omens and all the gods she knew. What was she thinking impersonating Lady Morina the Elder!

Wishing she had the cottage's magic to help with yet another deception, she made up her mind. "What is it, boy? Didn't Lady Morina tell you about the robbers on the road to Ravenshold? I'm the decoy for the lady. What, are you new here?"

She stuck out her chin. She could still channel the grumpy witch. It had worked well enough for her so far. And apparently her chalk-white hair and cottage-supplied garments were passable enough to assuage the boy.

"Oh, um," he began. "Right." Perhaps he *was* new here.

She nodded. "Go get the hatbox, boy, before your minute is up! I just needed to compare the lady's carriage to my own. I'll be leaving first."

"Of course," he muttered, scrunching his face up against the cold as he darted back toward the palace entrance.

Her heart thundering, she tossed the last of her viloil on the second carriage's harness and fled the stables, hoping the boy wouldn't mention anything about a decoy. Will needed a steel-clad way out of this marriage, and by all the gods and Omens, she was going to give it to him. It was the least she could do.

As she went to leave the way she had entered, she heard the shuffling of the boy again. He was carrying not one, but two hat boxes. She sunk into the shadows and out into the snow, her hood held fast about her face. No carriages or hooves followed her out of Wrestia, only the howling of the snowstorm. She had worried that the two women would simply ride their horses to meet the ridiculous feast requirement, but the snow had picked up, and from what she'd heard of the noble women's inclinations for comfort, they would clearly do no such thing.

Velina tucked away her chalk-white hair. Every step she took away from the icy city lifted her heart. She had done it—she had actually done something to help Will, all with the help of the cottage.

But when she reached the edge of the wood, the cottage was nowhere to be seen. Panic seized her, and her gaze swept the edge of the forest, searching for the smoking chimney and the dilapidated porch. Had Will left her? Had he taken the cottage back to Ravenshold and abandoned her here?

Spirits sinking, she hung her head. She deserved it. *More than* deserved it. After two nights of deception, she was certain the Omens deemed her worthy of abandonment in freezing cold Wrestia. At least the muck in this city's streets would be frozen if she was doomed to spend the rest of her life here.

But she stumbled on, stubbornly persevering

through the frozen wood seeking the cottage—her cottage. She had transformed it from a run-down shack to a cozy home, a home that would have taken her to Elody, where she would have finally been at ease. But at her own volition, she had shut the door on that sandy shore to go back and help Will. It was her own choice.

Just then, she stumbled on a rock hidden in the snowdrifts and went down on one knee, the icy sheet biting cold into her skin. She steadied herself on the rock and looked up to see the squat building swathed in snow. Relief melted in her chest.

Smoke rose merrily from the chimney, something she *should* have seen when she approached the wood. A light coating of snow rimmed the roof and walls. Had it been there all along? She shook her head, a smile blooming on her face at the mischievousness of the cottage. She was sure it had done this to her before, when she'd wandered around the same path in the Darkwood three times before it first appeared. *Three time's the charm, eh?*

Catching up the bottom of the fur cloak so she wouldn't trip, she dashed for the porch and entered the place she called home.

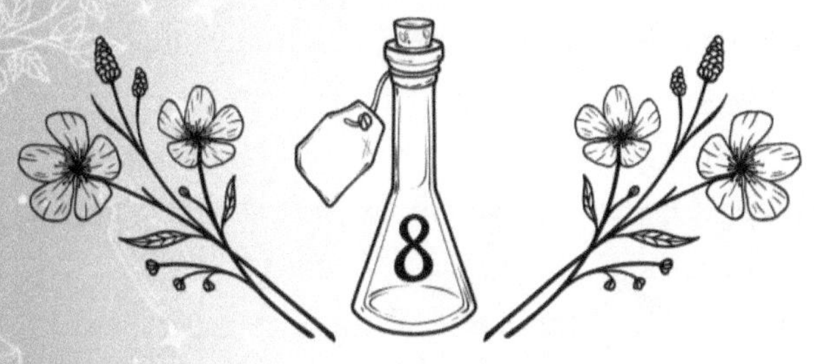

Three Weeks Later

"Open the door wider, will you?" Velina asked, awkwardly maneuvering her rocking chair out onto the porch. She really should just ask the cottage for more chairs that weren't as awkward to move. In the last few weeks, she had furnished the loft with a modest bedstead filled with plush blankets, added some soft carpets, and supplied herself with enough dishes and cups for the kitchen, and a tray for her tea pot, of course.

Silverweed dashed between her legs into the bright sunlight of the Elody beachside, nearly tripping her. Velina managed to get the chair and herself safely through the doorway. Will came through next with the second chair. He seemed a little more stable than her.

Velina donned her wide-brimmed straw hat and settled into her chair while Will ran back inside to grab their teacups. Silverweed was already rolling in the sand, a favorite pastime of his. Velina had finally given the cat a name, as he refused to leave the vicinity of the cottage no matter where they stopped to open the door. Of course, she thought she'd originally picked him up in the woods outside Ravenshold—the forest where she liked to forage—but Silverweed seemed content to stay with her. Or the cottage. She wasn't actually sure which he preferred.

The Ladies Morina of Wrestia never arrived for the wedding feast, and as a result, the marriage was nulled on the technicality. Will and his bees would remain in Ravenshold, his family none the wiser. Velina hoped to the Omens that his parents would consult him before attempting to arrange another marriage.

For herself, Velina was quite content to while away her days in the cottage on the edge of the wood. No matter where she opened her door, it was on the edge of the woods somewhere. Here in Elody, it was nestled under a thick patch of what Will called palm trees. Outside Ravenshold, it sat in the same place on the edge of the Ingwood just outside Will's holding. She just made sure to *never* think about Drĕghold or the Darkwood and to be as specific as possible before opening her door.

Since receiving the good news of his broken engagement, she and Will spent many an afternoon together. He even showed her his beehives on a particularly pleasant day. He went on and on about their upkeep, and the rate at which they produced honey, and how the wax was processed. She drank in the experience. She'd never *had* a friend to tell her about their hobbies before. They also spent several afternoons a week sipping tea on her front porch in the Ingwood—to ensure that she didn't accidentally ask the cottage to go anywhere else.

When she finally admitted her uncertainty about how the cottage worked and explained how she had stumbled upon it only recently, they decided to conduct a few experiments. Will had tried to use the cottage's magic when she was inside Wrestia, but it hadn't worked for him. So they spent hours testing everything. He couldn't get it to grant any of his wishes, whether she was inside or outside. She'd even chanced getting abandoned in the Ingwood once, when she shut him inside the cottage and asked him to try going somewhere else. He insisted that he had tried thoroughly to no avail. Only she could use it.

It was *hers*. She now had a home—here in Elody or wherever else she wanted to be. But in the recent weeks of joy at her newfound freedom, she'd already had another supplicant knock on her door looking for the witch. She had stopped in Harbrandt looking for a specific type of bee netting for Will, and the knock came just as Velina prepared to step out. Luckily, the petitioner only required an easy fix—a tonic for nerves. Will was teaching her how to read, since she'd asked the cottage for a book on medicinal plants, something she felt was the best way for her to grant "wishes" for real. She now knew magic was real, just not in the way she had expected.

But if that was who she had to be—a woman who

granted the simple wishes of desperate supplicants—
then so be it. Will theorized it was her faerŭn blood that
made the magic work.

She was the witch at the edge of the wood.

ACT II

THE WITCH

A few months later

A knock came at Velina's door.

That was how it always started. The door to her cottage still hung from the one hinge, though it was heavy enough to remain securely shut at times like these. She sat by the fire, her cauldron boiling away—a simple essence of lavender and virleek to make the cottage smell nice—and set her knitting down. She was making Will a scarf for his birthday next month. She'd never had a friend to give a birthday gift to, nor known how to knit until recently.

"Coming," she called, drawing a black silk scarf over her slightly pointy ears and covering her silver hair, which she had recently started keeping in a braid.

"I'm looking for the witch," the voice at the door said.

They always were.

Velina smirked. She often got callers after sundown, which was why she had already eaten her supper and put on the lovely-smelling tisane in her cauldron. No doubt she'd need to brew up a potion for whoever was outside. When she reached the door, she realized she was barefoot, however. *I need some black slippers*, she thought before adding, *please.* A pair of neat woolen slippers appeared on the floor before her, just her size. She slipped her feet into them, swishing her long green skirt over them like a twirling princess.

Thank you, she thought at the cottage. For it was the cottage that possessed all the magic, and not Velina. So, in what she felt was some measure of repayment for the home and ease the cottage provided her, she reached for the door to provide some sort of help for the person who sought out the witch.

The door groaned on its one hinge—no matter how she wished for it and despite all its magic, she couldn't fix the broken hinge. Several times she had asked for a replacement hinge and tools, which the cottage provided, and fixed it herself, only to find it broken or missing later. Apparently, that was one of the quirks of living in the witch's cottage at the edge of the wood.

"What is it?" she demanded when the door was a third of the way open. She held it there, remaining in the dim shadows. She found it best to be mysterious and gruff; people seemed disturbed when she acted her usual self. When they expected a witch, she had to give it to them. Anyway, she found it much more direct. No small talk. No dancing around their requests. Straight to the point so she could figure out their problem and provide a solution—which, since she herself didn't have any magic, was the tricky part.

"I...need your help," the woman on her porch said. Velina had heard the words a dozen times now since moving into the witch's cottage a few months ago.

"Yes, what is it?"

"Well," the woman said, "I came here looking for my cottage and found a girl living in it."

Velina's mouth gaped open. Well, that was straight to the point. "I..." she began.

The woman took advantage of her momentary shock and pushed the door farther open to bustle past. The dim moonlight outside revealed the lush woods near Ravenshold. Velina caught a whiff of smoke and mulberry as the woman's bloodred hood fell back to reveal pointy ears and straight silver hair.

"Y-you're—the witch?" Velina asked. The woman only looked about six or seven years older than her. She felt as if a heavy stone had dropped into her stomach. This was the very thing she had dreaded since first finding the cottage empty and spending the night here. She had long since assumed the real witch was dead.

Why would anyone leave such a magical place? Velina couldn't fathom a reason she would *ever* leave.

The woman's plump red lips curved into a smile. "I'm *a* witch, dearie. Much like you, eh?" She gestured around at the open cottage layout with the many cozy rugs, flowers, and decorations Velina had wished for since moving into the cottage. She'd asked for a soft sofa by the fire, a beautiful carved wooden table in the kitchen to prepare her meals, and more jars and canisters for the shelves. The cottage provided the herbs and plants she used for her potions, but she also enjoyed foraging for them herself. She even had a few plants growing in pots in the windowsill. It gave her something to do during the day. That, and perusing the pictures in the herbcraft books Will had loaned her, which he was slowly teaching her to read. They all came with illustrations, which was immensely helpful. "It seems you've made yourself at home."

"I-I-I'm so sorry," Velina stammered. Her short respite in the cottage came crashing down on her. She would have to say goodbye to the perks of the cottage answering her every whim and find somewhere else to live... Elody was still her first choice with its sandy beach and ever-present hush of waves caressing the shore, but it would be costly. It would also make it more difficult to visit Will. She could, of course, live in Ravenshold near him, but the city held a decade's-worth of bad childhood memories, from the orphanage to the workhouse. Her heart wrenched.

"Omens around us." The woman lingered in the kitchen nook. "Are you all right?"

Velina stood frozen by the door, all warmth drained from her face. "I'm...f..."

"Sit down," the woman said at once, and a cushioned chair appeared right behind Velina.

She collapsed into it. Of course, the woman could use the cottage—they were both faerǔn-touched. Will had reasoned that was why the magic worked for Velina while he couldn't use it.

"I'm just passing through, if that's what you're worried about," the woman said. She was bustling about in the kitchen nook with Velina's tea things.

"Oh?" Velina asked weakly. Now it felt like the heavy stone in her stomach had exploded. "Y-you're not here
to—"

"Take the cottage back?" the woman said with an arched eyebrow, teacup in hand. "Gods and Omens, no. I merely needed a—"

A knock at the door caused both of them to jump. It sounded less like a simple knock, and more like repeated pounding. The woman took a hasty sip of her tea and hissed, "I'm going to need you to get that. I'm not here."

er stomach writhing in knots, Velina shakily reached out to open the door for the second time that evening. The woman had disappeared up the ladder to the loft, which was sufficiently wreathed in shadows to hide her should the supplicant insist on coming inside. Velina's wits were scattered. She adjusted the black scarf hiding her ears and hair, then immediately checked it again.

After giving the dark loft a glance and spotting her cat bounding down the ladder—evidently roused from his early evening nap—Velina reached for the door handle and pulled it open a crack.

She held her jaw tight, still reeling. Who was the woman hiding in her loft? And what did she want if she truly didn't want to take back the cottage? Velina couldn't fathom why the older witch didn't want it; after only a few months with the cottage's magic, Velina never wanted to leave.

"What is it?" she demanded. She was no longer in any mood to entertain supplicants who needed tonics to make their warts go away or to curse their neighbor's crops to get back at them for winning the local harvest festival. She wanted to figure out who that faerŭn woman was.

"Rhymeris, I promise, it's not—oh—" The stranger stopped himself. He had a mop of chestnut brown hair falling into his eyes, which he flicked away with a practiced hand. "Rhymeris?"

Velina sighed, then looked up into his face, which was a head higher than hers. "Decidedly not. What is it that you need?"

"Well," he said in a low voice, slipping a hand in between the door and its frame and meeting her gaze, "I'm looking for my handsome lady friend." His voice grew husky, and Velina's shoulders crept up toward her ears. Was he...flirting with her?

"I wanted to tell her I was sorry I sprung that idea on her, and..." He tried to slip his hand farther inside, and on instinct, Velina nearly shut the door on his fingers.

"Ow!" She *had* shut it on his fingers. A bit.

"Finlowe!" The screeching admonishment came from the loft. "That isn't me, you fool!"

The man rescued his hand from the door, which Velina pulled open a few more inches. His mouth opened like a trout, and he stared past Velina to where Rhymeris was now climbing down from the loft, her red cloak fluttering around her legs. Velina allowed Rhymeris to bustle past her.

The woman pulled the door open wider. "Get in

here, you cad," she all but growled, slapping her hand on Finlowe's chest and grabbing a fistful of cloth by which to drag him good-naturedly inside, "before our young witch here has heart failure or someone actually looking for the witch comes by."

Velina blinked slowly as Rhymeris towed the man inside. "What in all the Omens is going on here?" she demanded, her high clear voice coming out more like a shriek than she intended.

Finlowe glanced at Rhymeris. The woman first narrowed her eyes at him, then patently ignored him as she explained, "I used to live here, as I was just beginning to tell you before I realized I had been *followed*. I thought I could just pass through to—"

"You weren't going to Drĕghold, were you?" Finlowe demanded, throwing a dramatic palm to his forehead in apparent annoyance. Rhymeris continued to ignore him. She cleared her throat and turned her whole body to face Velina, as if blocking him from the conversation would make him go away. He pouted, crossing his arms over his chest.

"As entertaining as this is..." Velina began.

"I know, I know," Rhymeris said, her attention wandering to the kitchen where she had left her cup of tea. The older girl then wandered to the kitchen to retrieve her cup. "I only came by because I wanted to pass through—you know it's like a gateway, right?" She pinned her eyes on Velina, who nodded with a grin. "Right. Sometimes I just use it to get to places when I don't feel like taking the roads."

"Really?" Velina put in. "But how come you don't live here anymore?"

Rhymeris shrugged. "I was done with it. Got sick of people knocking on my door all the time—that Omens-cursed half-broken door—and even though I could go anywhere I wanted in Viridia, I kind of got sick of still *being* in the same place, you know?"

Velina blinked. "I...can't even imagine. I mean, I was certainly sick of being in the workhouse. But this? Every day is like a dream."

Rhymeris gave Velina an appraising look over her teacup. "I thought you looked a bit starved. Spent some time in a workhouse myself."

Finlowe cleared his throat. "Met some pretty interesting people there, though, right?"

A wry smile twisted Rhymeris's lips. "Some hare-brained ones, perhaps. Oh! But where are my manners? What is your name, dearie?"

Velina bobbed her head and told them her name, then felt the need to embellish. "I only just came upon the cottage two months ago after escaping Drĕghold." Her face warmed. She had already told them about the workhouse—there was little else of her life story to tell.

"Velina," Finlowe said, sweeping the hair out of his eyes once more and offering her a charming smile. "I'm so sorry I mistook you for Rhymeris. I thought maybe she had disguised herself..." He trailed off. "I know there's some witchery about this place."

A rare smile bloomed on Velina's face. "It's all right. Do the two of you need a place to stay, or...?" She wasn't sure what to do. She'd never had any *real* guests besides Will, who came as often as he could escape his studies or his duties to his family's estate. And then, of course, there was that hive of bees he spent so much time taking care of. She hadn't seen him in over a week though; he was studying for some exam he didn't feel confident about, and his younger sister was out of town, so he had more family duties than usual.

"No, no—" Rhymeris began.

"Yes, actually—" Finlowe said at the same time.

Rhymeris cut him a glance. "You are not inflicting your awful plan on this poor girl. She's barely out of the workhouse, and she doesn't need you mucking up her life!"

Velina straightened her back. She could take care of herself. "What plan?"

Finlowe smiled and opened his mouth to speak, but Rhymeris spoke first. "Don't let him sugarcoat it. He wants to rob the Drĕgsons of Drĕghold."

11

The sound of waves ebbing and flowing over the night-dark beach gave Velina a sense of calm she had never known anywhere else. After receiving her guests' permission, she had asked the cottage to go to Elody and cracked open the door. It was what she did many a night, especially when she was agitated.

The door had to be cracked, because otherwise, no matter where she *thought* the cottage was, she couldn't hear any of the outside sounds. Once inside the cottage, it was as though she existed both nowhere and anywhere. But the open door was an anchor, and she reveled in the warm salty breeze that wafted in right along with the sound of the waves.

"So," Velina finally began, now that everyone was comfortably seated with a beverage of some kind. She didn't know much about entertaining guests, but that seemed to be the right thing to do. She had gotten some lavender tea to calm her nerves, but both Rhymeris and Finlowe had taken theirs with a healthy splash of brandy. "Why the Drĕgsons?"

Rhymeris heaved a sigh from where she had curled up on the other end of Velina's sofa. Velina still wasn't used to seeing the silver hair and ears on display so confidently. "You really need not get involved. I'm not about to."

Finlowe arched a brow at his friend. "I'll believe that when I see it." Then he addressed Velina. "They have something of value to the organization I'm a part of."

"Thieves," Rhymeris supplied.

He pretended to be offended. "Omens, no! How many times do I have to tell you? But if you *must* have me spell it out, Rhymeris, the Drĕgsons obtained this particular item by ill-gotten means themselves. So, rightfully, it's not theirs either."

Velina hid a smile behind her teacup before she took a sip. "I don't really need to know. I was just curious. I don't talk to too many people unless they need a tonic or something."

Rhymeris looked scandalized. "You don't...er...have any friends?"

"No, no, I do," Velina said hastily. "My friend Will has just been busy lately—"

She was glad Rhymeris cut her off, because her list of friends was already complete at exactly one. "You're doing the witch thing all wrong, dearie. Do you have any regulars yet? I had a few regulars I became friends with."

"Regulars?"

"People who need the same sort of potions and

repeat business?"

"Oh," Velina said. "No. That would be easier, though. I keep having to figure out what everyone needs, whenever they happen to knock on the door. Usually, I just tell them to come back the next evening. Then I spend the night looking up remedies." She gestured to the books stacked on the kitchen shelf.

Rhymeris waved a dismissive hand. "The remedies will come to you in time. That's what I always did. Throw some herbs in the cauldron—love yours, by the way...mine was this tiny copper thing...someone must have stolen it when I left it here—and you've got yourself a potion they think is magical, which, in the end, aren't all plants magic?" She smiled ruefully at Velina's wall of herb jars.

"But what you need are *regulars*. I used to have this little old lady outside of Myrindawn who would come by for her foot cream every Friday...and, well now that I think of it, making foot cream every week was perhaps one of the reasons that drove me to find alternate living quarters. So avoid agreeing to foot creams, actually."

Velina snorted into her tea. "I don't think I'd mind. I like helping people."

Rhymeris reached over and squeezed Velina's calf. "Of course you do, because no one helped you all your life, am I right?"

A sudden weight collapsed onto her chest, and Velina stared into the crackling fire. "I suppose."

"You're far more blessed by the Omens than I am," Finlowe offered, tossing back the remainder of his tea.

"I wouldn't give anything to anybody."

"Yes, in fact," Rhymeris said, "you prefer *taking*, do you not?"

Finlowe winked at Velina. "It's my way of getting back."

"And speaking of getting back," Rhymeris said, setting her teacup down on a small side table which hadn't been there a moment ago. "We should let Velina be. You and I can part ways outside of Ravenshold like we'd meant to."

"What?" Finlowe stood and pulled Rhymeris close, demanding in a low tone not meant for Velina's ears. "We're just going to leave her here to fend for herself? A young girl from the workhouse, here all alone?"

"She's getting along just fine," Rhymeris said at a normal volume. "Aren't you, dearie?"

"Oh, um, of course." Velina tried to look confident. Next to Rhymeris's striking beauty and poise, her own rendition fell a little flat.

Rhymeris narrowed her eyes. "How about I drop in tomorrow and become your first regular?"

HERBAL
REMEDIES

By the time the knock sounded on Velina's door several hours after dawn, she had gone through the cottage perhaps three times adjusting the decor. A new throw blanket was draped over the back of the sofa; she'd changed the curtains in the loft to blue, which bathed the whole cottage in a serene light from above; and the cauldron bubbled over the fire as usual, today with a few slices of hora citrus to liven up the air.

"Hi, hello," Velina said as she spied Rhymeris on the porch. The woman had her red hood up over her ears and hair but promptly lowered it upon entering.

"Where were you going to camp out today?" Rhymeris began.

"Camp out?" Velina asked, shutting the broken door with a practiced motion.

Rhymeris *tsked* as she headed to get a cup of tea, and then made a groan of utter delight. "Are these scones?" she asked incredulously. "You didn't figure out how to get the cottage to make food, did you?"

"No, no," Velina chuckled. "I went into the bakery in Elody first thing. It's one of the things I like to splurge on." Though her first instinct had been to save every single coin that came into her possession like a dragon hoarding his treasure, she had quickly decided that food—good food—was well worth the cost. And on one of her lonely days on the beach in Elody, she'd caught a waft of something delicious coming from the little boardwalk on the edge of the seaside village.

A feline grin spread across Rhymeris's face as she swiped a scone off the plate. They were hora citrus and clove, Velina's new favorite combination—they had also been the inspiration for her cauldron tisane this morning.

"Pastries are always worth splurging on," Rhymeris said sagely around a bite of crumbly dough.

"No Finlowe this morning?" Velina asked, eyeing the remaining scones. She'd already had one...and a half. She darted over to grab the second half—it was a done deal once she had started the thing, so she might as well not kid herself.

"No," Rhymeris said. "We parted ways last night. I love him, and he's fun to be around, but...some of his comrades convince him to take part in the stupidest schemes. And he just goes right along with it."

"So he's headed to Drěghold?"

"I suppose so."

"And what do you want to do here? I've got a few books on remedies my friend Will is helping me read, and—"

"No, I'm sure you'll figure out the remedies eventually. Though perhaps I should write down that foot cream recipe for you, just in case?" A glimmer in the girl's eye made Velina snort.

"Sure." She chuckled.

Rhymeris stuffed the last crumbs of the scone into her mouth, and a mint green cloth napkin appeared in her hands. She wiped her face neatly and tossed the napkin on the counter. "I used to keep the cottage in the same place each weekday, so for example, I spent every Myrsday in Ravenshold—that way the regulars could find me if needed, like I was saying last night. You do know, if the door is shut, you could be anywhere, right?"

Velina poured herself a new cup of tea to clear the crumbs stuck in her throat. "I was wondering about that," she said quietly. "Is that why I can't hear the waves in Elody unless the door is open?"

Rhymeris nodded. "The simple act of looking for the witch's cottage is what summons it to the edges of different woods. The petitioner must seek it out three times before finding it. You mean to tell me you just wait for *anyone* to knock from anywhere?"

Her face flooding with heat, Velina nodded.

"That's a recipe for disaster," Rhymeris said, leaning against the kitchen counter. "Pick a place for each day of the week. Or stay in just a few places. It's up to you. I wouldn't stay in one place all the time, however—it takes away from the mystique of the witch."

The way Rhymeris said *the witch* made her seem like a character from a storybook—a character both of them had played. She supposed that was exactly what this was. It was the witch's cottage, and Velina was the witch now.

"I still can't believe you left this place," Velina blurted out.

A sad smile turned up Rhymeris's lips, and she said, "Eventually, you might want to leave it too, and that's all right. Or you might choose to spend all your days here. You have to find your own way, dearie. But if you want to do this well, make sure you don't burn yourself out answering every single call from everywhere the door might open to."

Velina nodded. "You're right. I didn't realize the knocks could come from anywhere." She shivered. "I really don't want anyone from Drĕghold finding me. The foreman at the workhouse—he chased me through the Darkwood once. That was actually how I found out the cottage door opened anywhere..." She went on to tell Rhymeris about Eghrŭn and everything that had happened with Will after.

Rhymeris let out a lyrical chuckle as Velina finished her story. "So this Will was your first patron, then?"

"I just *had* to help him," Velina said with a shrug.

"Where do you want to go today?"

"How about Ravenshold?" After all the talk of Will, she was missing her friend.

"You're the witch," Rhymeris said, spreading her palms wide.

Velina grinned. She was so relieved that Rhymeris didn't want the cottage back and was going so far to help her. This was the happiest she'd been in a long time. Maybe ever.

Please take me to Ravenshold, she asked the cottage. That was where she had picked up Rhymeris from this morning, but now she knew that from the moment she closed the door, the cottage could be anywhere. She waited a few seconds, then opened the door to peek out. The forest that greeted her was verdant and lively. She could see a frolicking chipmunk from here, bounding through lyrberry bushes that were heavy with fruit— definitely the lush Ingwood outside Ravenshold.

"Now, crack the door like you did last night," Rhymeris instructed. "I suspect that's why the hinge won't fix. I must have tried a thousand times."

A chuckle burst from Velina's lips as she closed the door so that only a sliver of light shone through the crack. "Me too. So now the cottage can't be found in other places?"

Rhymeris shook her head. "Nope. It might take a few weeks to gain some regulars though, since you'll have less people knocking on your door each day. It can get boring."

"I don't think I'll ever get bored of this."

"I hope not," Rhymeris said softly. "It seems like it gives you joy. We must find joy where we can get it, eh dearie? And when you can't find it, make it." She winked and settled down on the arm of the sofa.

Velina pressed her lips tight and nodded. "I like

helping people. No one ever wanted to even speak to me before, with the—" She gestured at her hair and ears.

Eyes narrowed, Rhymeris studied her. "There's nothing wrong with us, you know. In fact, I would argue we are more special than others, considering we can use the magic of this place."

"Do you know...anything about the faerŭn?" Velina asked in a quiet voice.

Rhymeris glanced at her out of the corner of her eyes. "I grew up in an orphanage like you. But I don't think that means we were swapped at birth by some magical people. I think our parents were afraid, and fear can drive even the best people to do stupid and horrible things."

Silverweed hopped down from the loft ladder at that moment, padding over to curl around Velina's leg. Velina remained quiet for a few minutes, processing what Rhymeris had said and trying to reconcile it with her feelings about her past. She had never spared much anger toward whoever had abandoned her; she had been too full of fear for her own existence. Now, she just felt pity for her parents.

"What do we do now? With the cottage," she clarified.

"Now we wait!" Rhymeris said. "I used to have friends over or spend the time mixing tinctures. Once you know what you'll need more frequently, that can help you pass the time. You don't want to go making too much foot cream that will go bad when no one asks for it," she added with a sly look.

"I'm starting to wonder if you *liked* making that foot cream," Velina jested.

Rhymeris roared with laughter, drawing Velina's lips into a smile. She didn't think she'd ever made anyone laugh like that before. "Fine, fine, let's get it out of the way, and I'll show you how to make the Omens-blessed foot cream. You can always use it on yourself if nobody comes looking for it!"

The older girl wrote down the recipe, but Velina could only make out a few words with her limited reading skills, so she committed it to memory while Rhymeris added the ingredients to various glass containers. The smell of melting beeswax by the fire made Velina think of Will and his bees.

Just before Velina was about to suggest she start something for dinner, a knock came at the cottage door. She shared an excited look with Rhymeris, who at once vaulted up into the loft to lurk in the shadows. Silverweed was again ousted by the newcomer invading his space, and he hopped down the last of the ladder's rungs to join Velina by the door.

"Hello?" a voice said from outside. "I'm looking for the witch."

Velina smiled down at the cat. She found it amusing how everyone always said the same thing. Perhaps that was part of the cottage's magic...or simply the default phrase that jumped to people's minds. She reached up to secure her scarf on her head and pulled open the door.

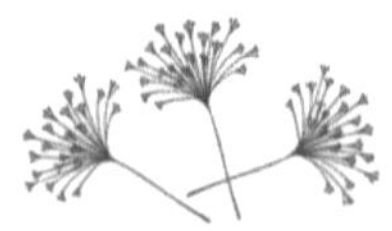

And so it went for the next week. Rhymeris claimed she had nothing better to do while Finlowe executed his ill-conceived robbery—Rhymeris's exact words—and came every morning, meeting Velina outside of Ravenshold. Velina suspected the scones also enticed the faerŭn girl; Velina continued to spend her nights in Elody and, first thing in the morning, set out on the sandy shore for the bakery on the boardwalk.

They asked the cottage to go to a different wood each day. Despite Rhymeris's insistence that Velina needn't figure out all the remedies at once, the girl seemed to light up each time she suggested one to Velina, and she insisted on showing Velina how to make each of them. When a patron in Melodïgha knocked, Velina had a chance to learn about the actual use of blackfork leaves—it was not something that would have gotten Will out of a marriage, and she most certainly would have poisoned him by preparing it wrong. Rhymeris showed her how to brew them into a noxious-looking potion that in fact tasted like blackberries and imbued the drinker with a sense of calming happiness. Velina was incredibly impressed that a simple herb could accomplish such a thing, and wondered why everyone wouldn't drink it all the time. Rhymeris, of course, pointed out the various strainers and tweezers they'd used to make it non-lethal, as the tiny spines lining the leaves were deadly sharp. The cottage made preparing the leaves feasible. It also took all day to brew, and it only resulted in two small vials of the tincture.

When a quiet gentleman knocked in Fehrgarde, Velina consulted Rhymeris on how she could possibly grant a wish to dampen background noise.

"I can't take it," the man had said, his voice low. "I feel like I'm crazy, Mistress Witch, but I can't stand the sounds all the time. People hacking their spit into the street. And worse, worse! The mongrels who chew with their mouths open in the tavern. I feel like I'm going mad."

Velina had asked the man to return later that evening, giving him a small vial of the blackfork infusion to try in the meantime.

"That's a tough one," Rhymeris said, flipping through Velina's herbcraft book. She made a face, then held out her hand. Another book appeared there, cherry red binding with gold lettering that Velina couldn't read. "I used to use this book myself. *Pepper's Plants and Potions*. I liked the alliteration."

She tossed the new book into Velina's lap. Velina lifted it carefully and began flipping through it, staring at all the illustrations of plants with their detailed drawings of roots, stems, and stamens. But her reading lessons with Will had taken a hiatus while he was busy, and she could only read a few words here and there.

"What is it?" Rhymeris asked, keen eyes studying her.

"I...um... I can't read," Velina admitted. "Will was teaching me, but..."

"Ah, I see. Well, I'll bookmark the best ones, shall I?"

Not only did Rhymeris bookmark her favorites, but she read through them with her, pointing out words and adding her own commentary. Velina did her best to memorize what she could.

"What about this one?" Rhymeris asked after marking half a dozen useful recipes. "Calms nerves. Quiets inner turmoil. Uses ffrey root."

Velina leaned over to see the illustration Rhymeris was pointing at. "Ffrey root? I've never seen it before. That does sound promising though. Calm and quiet?"

I wish I had a jar of ffrey root, she thought. They both glanced down at the glass jar now sitting on the table beside them, containing three sections of a purplish-brown root.

"Let's get this brewed up before your gentleman comes back, shall we?" Rhymeris asked. "I bet he becomes a regular in no time."

When it came time to bring the cottage to Elody for a day, Velina cracked the door to hear the waves, a grin lighting up her face. The palm trees swayed in the breeze, making the fan-shaped shade on the porch constantly morph into different forms.

She had brewed a dozen new potions in the last few days and was beginning to recognize some of the smaller words Rhymeris pointed out in the books. She was memorizing the recipes, but she looked forward to browsing the books like Rhymeris did—stumbling across just the perfect herb for the situation as she researched.

"I might do two days a week in Elody," she confessed as she went to sit on the sofa beside Rhymeris. Since Velina never wanted to visit Drĕghold again, and she'd had no callers at all in Vidgarde, she thought she'd experiment with different places until she found a comfortable schedule. She was quite looking forward to not having fate decide where she opened her door, now that she realized that was an option.

"It is lovely here," Rhymeris agreed. "Though I could do without the sand in my boots."

Velina tucked her bare feet under her skirt. "That's why I don't wear shoes on the beach," she chuckled. "Does the feverfew tincture look ready to you?"

Rhymeris inspected the bottles lined up on the

workspace table Velina had asked the cottage for. It had a nice flat wooden surface with plenty of compartments and drawers for all the tools she'd acquired throughout her potion-making. She'd finished decanting the feverfew late last night with the sound of the waves playing their symphony in the background.

"They're perfect. You really can't overdo it with feverfew."

A creak on the porch outside alerted them to a visitor before the knock came.

The person sounded out of breath. "Velina! Are you in there?"

"**W**ill?" Velina demanded incredulously, striding to the door. "But we're in Elody...*aren't we?*" She yanked open the wonky door, revealing her friend and the sandy shore behind him. "What in the name of the Omens are you doing *here?*"

"I couldn't find you! The cottage didn't appear in the Ingwood for the last few days!" He crashed into her, throwing his arms around her.

Velina froze, not sure what to do with her hands. She had seen people hug before, but was it normally so painful? She felt as if her chest would collapse. Tentatively, she put her hands on Will's shoulders. "I'm fine, I was just trying something new..."

"This is Will, eh?" Rhymeris said from the edge of the loft, her legs hanging over the ladder.

Will released Velina and stared up in shock at Rhymeris, whose hair and ears were on full display. He glanced between the two of them. "I-I-tried to find you, and I thought you might be here. I *hoped* you were here. My sister's gone missing. Merrylyn was visiting

Drĕghold with her academic cohort and hasn't returned."

Acid burned Velina's throat. "I'm so sorry, Will!" she gushed. "I've been keeping the cottage in one place all day—different places. I never thought... If you needed me—"

"It's not your fault," Will said. "I just thought with both of you missing—I didn't know what to think. And if anyone could help—"

"Have you been to Drĕghold already?"

He nodded, setting his satchel by the door and taking a few more steps inside, shooting a quick glance at Rhymeris. "Yes, of course. I came straight here after I spoke to the Drĕgsons."

Velina looked at Rhymeris. "The Drĕgsons?" she asked with meaning.

Rhymeris set her mouth in a thin line. "Finlowe better not have anything to do with this," she growled.

"Quick, I can bring the cottage to Drĕghold—" Velina began.

Will held up a hand. "But what about Swarm?"

"Sw—?" Rhymeris started.

"His horse," Velina explained, leaning over to catch sight of the buckskin mare outside on the sand, her gorgeous golden coat and black hair reminding her of Will's bees. "Erm...do you think she'd...come inside the cottage?" She looked questioningly at Rhymeris to gauge how ridiculous she thought the idea was.

The older girl shrugged. "I've never tried it, but I don't see why not."

"Are you..." Will hesitated. "Another witch?"

"Witch, faerŭn...same thing." Rhymeris shrugged. She hopped down from the ladder and came over to the two of them. "Name's Rhymeris. I lived here for a few years before Velina took over."

Will's mouth popped open in surprise. "Pleasure to meet you. I'm Will, a friend of Velina's. I don't think Swarm has ever fit through a normal door before, but we can try."

It turned out Swarm would not even try, so it didn't matter whether she could fit or not.

"I'm sorry, Will," Velina said, after she watched him lead the mare back down the single step from the porch. The horse had only gotten her two front feet up onto the porch before rebelling against their admittedly insane plan.

"It's not your fault," he said.

"Can you leave her to roam the beach? Would she go far?" Rhymeris suggested.

He shook his head. "She would either run off or tear up whatever tree I tied her to. I don't know how long we might be gone, either. I guess I can ride her to Drĕghold and meet you there tomorrow?" His eyes crinkled in worry.

Velina frowned. "No, there has to be a better way. If something happened to your sister... Oh! I know. What if I go to the bakery and ask if they know of any stables in Elody? Would she be content in an unfamiliar stable? It's a small town, but there might be something."

Will thought it over for a second, his hand going to Swarm's golden flank. Then he nodded. "I think that's our best bet."

Velina hurried inside to ask the cottage for her sandals, which she'd left in the loft. Sandals in her hand, she hopped off the porch and joined Will on the sand. She glanced back at the cottage, frowning. She always felt nervous leaving it empty. When she'd left Will in Wrestia, she hadn't known he couldn't use the cottage's magic, but she knew for certain Rhymeris could. A nagging worry made her say, "Rhymeris, why don't you come with me? I'll show you where I buy those scones you love so much. Will, you stay here and make sure the cottage doesn't go anywhere. Just keep the door cracked."

Velina grabbed Swarm's reins and waited for Rhymeris to hop down from the porch. The two of them covered their heads and set off across the sand with a wave back at Will.

After a few minutes of their fast-paced walk down the beach, which was getting increasingly sunny the farther they got from the cottage and its overhanging palm trees, Rhymeris slyly commented, "I thought you realized I wasn't going to steal your cottage from you."

Velina's face flamed. She opened her mouth to speak, but merely closed and opened it a few times when no words came out.

Rhymeris elbowed her. "It's fine, Velina. I would have done the same thing. But I want you to know what I said was true. I'm not here to take it from you. It's *your* home now. The cottage is a gift. I had my time with it already."

Velina swallowed the huge lump in her throat. "I... Thank you." She didn't say anything else until the quaint boardwalk of Elody came into view. Between Will's sister gone missing and Rhymeris's friendship with Finlowe, an admitted thief, Velina's walls had started to go back up. Swarm ambled along peacefully on the sand behind them, the reins loose in Velina's hand.

"I'm sorry," Velina said. "It's just I've never...had any reason to trust *anyone*."

"I am not offended," Rhymeris said pointedly. "And though you should certainly guard your trust like the prized possession that it is, you *are* allowed to let people in sometimes. Like you clearly have with Will."

Velina nodded, then pointed to the first building along the boardwalk. "There it is. Quincy's Creams." Unbidden, her mouth watered. But now was not the time for creampuffs, which were painted expertly on the shop's sign.

Rhymeris waited outside holding Swarm's reins, and the bell above the door rang when Velina stepped inside.

The girl at the counter looked up. She appeared around Velina's age, give or take a year. Velina often saw her bringing trays of pastries from the kitchen, while Mr. Quincy manned the counter.

"Hello," Velina said nervously, adjusting her black scarf. "Is Mr. Quincy here?"

The girl shook her head. She had bronze curls and striking honey-colored eyes like her father, the resemblance so strong that Velina didn't doubt their relation for a second. "He always takes off upstairs after the morning rush to go lie down with a cup of tea and one of his novels," she explained, a light Elody brogue in her accent.

"Ah," Velina said, twisting her fingers together, now less certain of this brilliant plan of hers. She had hoped Mr. Quincy would be here, considering he was the one who took her money every morning.

"Is there something I can help you with? You've been coming in a lot lately. You new to Elody?"

"Um, yes," Velina said. "Maybe you can help. It's sort of a strange request. I have a friend who needs to board his horse for the day—maybe overnight? And I don't have anywhere convenient or know anywhere nearby..."

"Oh," the girl said. "The tavern's down at the other end of the boardwalk, and they're bound to have posts to lend. How long do you need to leave her?"

"I don't actually know," Velina admitted. "It could be a few days."

The girl put a finger to her chin, pensive. The smudge of flour ruined her thoughtful expression a bit. "We have the old barn in the back. It *is* empty. Used to get our own flour with the donkey cart, but now we get it delivered."

"Would that be..." Velina began. "I mean, I wouldn't want to put you out. I'll pay you."

"Nonsense!" The girl chuckled. "You're our best new customer. Why my father was just saying he wanted to introduce himself, but you didn't talk much, and I—I talk a lot, actually. What's your name, anyway?"

"Velina. And you are?"

"Fionagh Quincy, at your service." She reached out a hand dusted in flour and marred by a few burns, which Velina shook gratefully.

"I'm going to be out of town for a few days," Velina said, reaching into her pocket. "Consider this payment for either the horse boarding or the scones I would have gotten."

elina was quiet as they walked back to the cottage. Having found a secure place for Will's beloved stead—where Fionagh had already begun to care for the animal—the prospect of going back to Drĕghold was beginning to sink in.

Drĕghold. The place she'd vowed to never again return.

When she stepped inside and shut the half-broken door, she couldn't find it in herself to ask the cottage to move. Without meeting anyone's eyes, she went up into the loft.

Downstairs, Rhymeris inquired if Will needed anything. The girl then asked the cottage for another cloak and showed him where the leftover pastries were. Velina heard them talking quietly about his day-long ride from Drĕghold, and guilt seized her stomach as she hid in the shadows of the loft, clutching her abdomen as if she had a real stomachache.

She didn't have to go anywhere near the workhouse. She owed Eghrŭn nothing, despite anything his ledger might say. She knew she didn't possess nearly enough money to "pay back" what she "owed," but the fear of being physically taken off the streets pervaded her mind. She had turned her back on that workhouse months ago, when she'd traded her last meal for a cryptic map from a traveling tinker. All to find the witch.

To become the witch.

Silverweed meowed lazily from Velina's bed. He had curled up next to her pillow as usual. She sank down next to him and ran a hand along his back. *I can do this,* she thought to herself. *I have to help Will. That's what friends do.*

No longer did she feel as if she owed him—they had both agreed that her ruse as the witch in the beginning had been paid off by her getting him out of that marriage—but the strength of her compulsion to help, simply because he was her friend, was new to her.

She gathered a large sum of coins into a pouch and slid it securely into her skirt pocket. Then, she asked the cottage for a dagger.

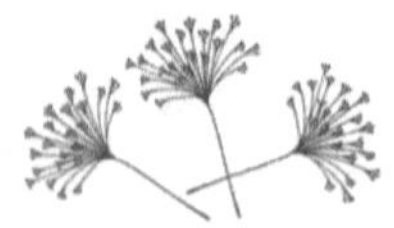

Despite the sheathed dagger in her right pocket and coins in her left, fear still ran through her when she stepped out into the Darkwood, Will and Rhymeris at her heels. The last time she'd been here, Eghrŭn had pursued her through the trees. And before that, she'd made a hasty retreat from Drĕghold, then wandered desperately, thinking she was lost and would never find the place.

But as she looked back on the cottage, she found the sight bolstered her courage. Silverweed had slunk out to sit on the porch, and he watched them leave with a bored expression. Velina silently sent the cat a goodbye, bidding him to watch over the place.

"You know," Rhymeris said, coming up next to her, "the cottage never left me behind before—ever. You found it when it was abandoned. That's how I found it too. I think it knows when it has an owner and remains loyal to them."

Velina nodded. That was what she feared second-most about returning to Drĕghold. Her foremost fear confronted her as soon as they crossed the pike fence. Beggars on the mud-caked streets lingered down alleyways, from old men to young kids, all with a layer of dirt on them, much like the doorways and stairs they loitered on. She never wanted to go back to that life.

Velina clutched the sheathed dagger tighter but didn't avert her gaze and kept walking. "To the Drĕgsons'?" she asked Will.

"We could, but they didn't have any idea what happened. The rest of the academic cohort returned to Ravenshold—it was a week-long trip to the conservatory."

"The conservatory, then?"

Rhymeris put a hand on Velina's stiff arm. "I'm going to go find Finlowe, if that's all right with you. In case he knows anything."

Velina nodded. "That's a good idea." She didn't know how a twelve-year-old girl visiting the conservatory could get caught up in a theft from the Drĕgsons' estate, but it was worth a shot. "Where should we find you?" Velina asked.

"I have a feeling he's in West Drĕghold, so I'm going there."

It was the most dangerous part of the city, where the workhouses stood. Velina shivered. "Omens be with you," she said, giving the girl's hand a squeeze. "Worst case, we meet back at the cottage, all right?"

Velina checked that her headscarf was secure before they parted ways, and she and Will headed in the direction of the clock tower at the center of Drĕghold.

"Merrylyn's friends didn't know anything about what happened?" Velina asked. "She wasn't getting forced into a marriage, was she?"

"No, no," Will said, sounding worried. "And she's not the type to run away. Here, the conservatory is down this way, across from the clock."

Velina was surprised to see cobblestones lining the central square of Drĕghold; she'd thought the whole city consisted of muddy streets. She had spent most of her time in West Drĕghold, however.

The two of them turned down Aria Street and were immediately confronted with a massive three-story building with columns at the front, flying buttresses coming out the sides, and a looming belltower high in the blue sky. Velina stopped in her tracks. It took up an entire city block.

"Wh-what—is that the conservatory?" she demanded.

"Um, yes," Will said, looking up at it.

"And your sister was staying there for a whole week to learn about…"

"Music."

"Music?" Velina asked, shocked. She had never seen such finery or heard of something so fantastically fanciful. And to think, all her life she'd only ever seen the muddy underside of these cities. She was starting to see why Rhymeris had wanted to leave the cottage, if places like this existed. "That's *incredible*."

Will pressed his lips into a thin smile. "Well, it *was* incredible."

Reality slapped her out of her reverie. "Right. Let's head in and see if there's any news."

The headmaster at the conservatory met with them right away, giving an odd glance at Velina's covered head—she looked almost like the Mosu nuns in Ravenshold—then filling them in on the search for Merrylyn.

Velina sat and listened, watching Will. He stared at the headmaster's desk without blinking. When they left the unproductive meeting, she put a hand on his arm. This seemed to jar him.

"Why don't we walk the streets a bit?" she asked, looking up and down the beautiful cobblestoned road.

"Maybe ask around?"

Will went along with her suggestion quietly, kicking his feet along the cobbles.

"What did your parents say, anyway?" she demanded after they'd passed only a few houses. Will muttered something about ensuring they'd hold the Drĕgsons responsible, and how Merrylyn would surely turn up eventually with everyone looking for her.

On the other side of the street, a man was walking in the same direction as them. Velina studied the man, confident it wasn't anyone she knew from the workhouse. Though he did look a little familiar...

Wait a minute... She tugged on Will's arm and led him across the street, narrowly avoiding a carriage that was trundling down the way.

"What is it?" Will hissed. She shushed him and made sure her hood was secure as she hurried along.

The man glanced back, his face shaded by a hood, then he picked up his pace.

She dropped Will's arm when the man rushed down an alley. "Finlowe!" Velina hissed when they were inside the alley. "I knew it!"

He whirled around in surprise, nearly dropping the satchel he'd been clutching to his chest. "Oh!" He visibly relaxed into a slumped posture. "It's the little witch. I thought...well, it doesn't matter. What in the Omens are you doing out of your cottage?"

Velina narrowed her eyes at his satchel. Obviously, Finlowe was up to something unsavory. She nodded at Will. "My friend's sister went missing from the music conservatory. Will, this is a friend of Rhymeris."

"Oh? Oh no," Finlowe's voice pitched funny.

"You haven't been by the conservatory, have you?" she said, an eyebrow raised. He *had* been coming from that direction.

He cleared his throat. "Course not. I've no interest in their stuffy music. Prefer a lively tavern ballad, if you ask me."

"Uh huh. Have you seen Rhymeris? She went to West Drĕghold looking for you, actually. To help us find Will's sister."

"Rhymeris is in Drĕghold too?" His eyes darkened. "Omens, she shouldn't be here."

"Why not?"

Finlowe lowered the satchel, finally looping it over his shoulder and pinning them with a look. "Come to think of it, *you* shouldn't be here either, little witch. I heard the workhouses are on a rampage, scooping up faerŭn left, right, and center—"

Velina gasped, a hand going to her throat. "Eghrŭn. I bet he's behind this. He's furious I got away, and— why would he take other faerŭn, though?"

"Why indeed," Finlowe said. "Here, let's get you off the streets. Why don't you two come with me? Actually, would you mind carrying this, little witch? You'd be doing me a favor." Velina lowered her chin and crossed her arms, sure he had something he wasn't supposed to and only wanted her to carry it so he would look less suspicious. He pretended to shiver. "Rhymeris must be giving you scary faerŭn witch lessons. Look, it's nothing dangerous, I promise. Just a relic that needs a new home. And to think, the Drĕgsons thought it was a musical instrument..." He trailed off.

"Fine," Velina said, shaking her head. "Can we go find Rhymeris, though? I'm worried they could have—" Her voice hitched.

"We'll head to the Merry Monk," he said, handing the satchel to her.

She took it reluctantly but, at this point, found she didn't care. She just wanted to get going. The satchel with its mysterious item looped over her shoulder, she grabbed Will's arm and pulled him after Finlowe.

As they walked, she asked Will under her breath, "Do you want to keep searching the streets, or do you mind going with Finlowe? He's a bit shady, but he's also friends with Rhymeris."

Will eyed the satchel. "I don't have a better plan. And we should find Rhymeris if they're rounding up faerŭn. Maybe she's heard something, or someone at the tavern knows something."

Velina stared straight ahead, watching Finlowe's progress in her peripheral vision. "Right."

She hoped to the Omens that Rhymeris was all right. If Eghrŭn had taken her, he'd pay for it.

etween the smell coming from the tannery and the downtrodden faces of anyone they passed on the street, be it urchins in doorways or workers hustling down the muddy road, Velina could tell they were in West Drĕghold. The cobblestones had also disappeared several blocks back.

Will sniffed and moved closer to Velina. Finlowe had dropped back to walk near her as well. She knew what they were doing. She reached into her pocket to feel for her sheathed dagger. If the time came, would she use it?

Luckily, the Merry Monk wasn't much farther. Finlowe pushed the door open with a stiff arm, beckoning Velina and Will inside. Velina couldn't help but look around the moment she crossed the threshold. Everything, from the walls to the tables and even the mugs adorning them, seemed to be made of wood—everything except the stone hearth, which crackled merrily beside a pair of orcs trading stories over the card game of virnolz laid out on their table. Finlowe made some signal with his hand to the curvy older woman behind the massive wooden bartop, and she bustled off somewhere in response.

The windows were grimy, but candles littered every table, contributing to the black residue on the glass. Half a dozen customers were sampling from their wooden cups and people were either talking in low voices or shouted responses—there was no in between.

There was also no sign of Rhymeris.

"Have you ever...been to a tavern?" Will asked her, looking pointedly at her open jaw. She shut it with haste and shook her head.

"They're all pretty much the same," Finlowe chimed in. "Though none's got a barkeep as friendly as this one. Cheers, Dahl." He accepted three wooden mugs from the woman who'd come out from behind the bar, and then she leaned close to whisper something in Finlowe's ear. He bobbed his head once, and the barkeep retreated back to her post without another word. Finlowe shepherded them to a corner table away from the windows, and Velina made sure her head was covered as she always did.

Two stubby candles burned on their table, guttering a little as the three swept into their seats and Finlowe set down the mugs. "Nothing from Rhymeris," he reported, taking a long swig of his drink.

Will took a tentative sip and made a face. That was enough to discourage Velina, who'd only ever seen the aftereffects of too much drink when the foremen at the workhouses got sick. She pushed hers toward Finlowe, who didn't seem to notice or care.

"I wish we knew where Rhymeris was," Velina said. "And Merrylyn. I don't want to spend any more time in this city." She dropped her hands onto her lap in frustration, and they landed on Finlowe's satchel. It was then that she felt something move inside the satchel.

She yanked her hands back from the bag. "What in—Finlowe," she hissed. "What is in this bag?"

He cast her a confused glance. "It's just a trinket—nothing to be worried about."

Nothing to be worried about? She had sworn the item inside had settled at the bottom of the bag, some kind of long item like a heavy stick. And now it was turned in an entirely different direction. She didn't want to deal with this. She just wanted to find Rhymeris.

The object jerked again—more forcefully this time—as if the point was being drawn by a magnet toward the fireplace. Eyes wide, she lifted the flap on the bag, her other hand hovering in case the object decided to fly out. *What a crazy idea*, she thought. But since she had moved into a magic cottage that granted her every wish, nothing seemed crazy anymore.

Keeping the flap of the bag over the object—she didn't want to reveal the stolen item, nor did she want anyone in the tavern to see whatever strangeness was occurring in her lap—she peered inside. Finlowe had frozen with his mug halfway to his lips, and Will was eyeing her warily. Inside the bag was a thin metal rod a little shorter than her forearm. The surface was engraved with runes and covered in delicate silver filigree. One end had a point like an arrow, which was currently aimed in the direction of the fireplace like a needle on a compass.

She blinked at it. "Finlowe," she said in a low voice, "what in the Omens is this thing? It *moved.*"

He opened his mouth, shut it, and opened it once more. "I had heard the legends, but I never really thought... I had hoped maybe..."

Velina exchanged incredulous looks with Will, who was bobbing his foot nervously where it rested across his knee. *Poor Will. He just wants to find his sister. I wish we knew where she was.* The intricate metal thing in the bag shifted a little.

Velina's eyes bulged. "I think...I think... No, it's not possible."

"What?" Will demanded in a half-whisper.

"I think it might be trying to tell me where they are," she whispered.

I wish I knew where the barkeep of the Merry Monk was, Velina thought.

The rod twitched in the opposite direction, pointing toward the back room of the tavern, where Velina had seen the barkeep go only a few moments ago.

After asking Finlowe a few pointed questions, they'd been able to sort out the nature of what Finlowe had called the faeryn rod. *I wish I knew where the front door of the Merry Monk was*, she thought. It swiveled to point directly toward the door.

"That proves it," she said triumphantly.

The magic was familiar, similar to the cottage's magic, but it provided direction not things.

Finlowe watched her, enraptured.

"Why did you 'acquire' this thing, anyway?" she asked.

His face flushed. "May I?" he asked, holding out a hand.

"Oh! Of course," Velina said, passing it to him under the table.

He put it in the shadow of his arm on the tabletop, his face going slack as he concentrated. Velina watched Will tapping out a rhythm with his foot on his knee. Just as she was about to suggest they continue their search, Finlowe looked up at Velina, disappointment clearly written across his face. Understanding dawned on Velina.

"It might only work for—" she began.

"Faerŭn," Finlowe supplied mechanically. "I thought that might be a possibility after hearing about this, and after Rhymeris told me how the cottage worked."

"Let's get going," Velina said, pulling Will's sleeve. He was all too eager to jump to his feet and lead the way to the door.

Outside, in the shadow of the doorway, Velina replaced the faeryn rod in the satchel, holding the flap open so she could see inside. "I wish I knew where Merrylyn Ravenson is," she said aloud, for the benefit of the others. The rod pivoted, pointing to the northwest.

"Is she even in Ravenshold still?" Will demanded. The city didn't extend much farther to the northwest, and there was no reason she should be in West Drĕghold anyway.

"Hold on, let me check something else. I wish I knew where Rhymeris is."

The rod moved only slightly. If she hadn't been watching it keenly, she wouldn't have known it had moved at all. So that must mean...

"They're close by each other?" Will surmised. "What's out that way?"

"Eghrŭn's workhouse, for one," Velina whispered.

To Velina's surprise, they didn't set off right away. And it was Will, of all people, who suggested they go back inside the Merry Monk. Brow furrowed, Velina started to comply, until she realized what he was doing.

"No, I'm coming with you," she blurted out. "I have to!"

"You don't have to," Will said. "Really. I know you never wanted to step foot in Drĕghold again, and here I am dragging you right back to the very door—"

"But we don't actually *know* they're at the workhouse," she argued. She didn't know why she was arguing *for* going to the workhouse, only that Rhymeris and Merrylyn needed help. And Velina found herself in a position to give it.

Had anyone helped *her* in all those years she'd spent under the heel of those bigger and more powerful than her? No. And it was for that very reason Velina knew in her bones that she would help Rhymeris and Merrylyn and anyone else she could. "Look, you came to me for help finding Merrylyn. Well, this is how I help. And besides," she went on, "you need me to use the faeryn rod."

Finlowe watched their conversation without interrupting, the corner of his lower lip between his teeth. He evidently didn't want to get involved, but as he tapped his fingers on his crossed arms, she could tell he wanted to get going. It was clear that he and Rhymeris had a history, and Velina suspected his feelings ran deep.

"Let's just get closer," Velina said. "Come on."

Will followed, a cloud of worry evident around him. He gave up the pretense of walking close to her and simply hooked her arm in his elbow like he was a gentleman leading her to tea. She obliged and let him, if that was what would make him feel better about it.

A surprising smile brought up the corners of her lips as she made a mental note to let Will bring her to tea someday. Ever since inheriting the cottage, she hadn't wanted to leave her sanctuary, except for brief jaunts to the bakery or to find Will at his castle. He had, of course, wanted to introduce her to his bees. But there would be time for tea after they found the girls.

Velina kept up a stream of thoughts aimed at the faeryn rod, lifting the bag's flap periodically to see where it pointed. The rod was entrancing—the way it moved on its own and responded to thoughts and wishes just like the cottage did.

As they trod deeper down the muddy streets of West Drĕghold, Velina wondered at the faerŭn magic. Everything she'd discovered so far was powerful and amazing. So why did everyone shun those with faerŭn blood? She shook her head. She would never understand the workings of the world.

She alternated between asking about the two girl's names, just in case they weren't together. But with the miniscule changes to the rod when she switched requests, it seemed they were in close proximity. And as she continued along the recognizable path, a familiar pit opened in her stomach. She was certain she knew where they were, despite what she had told Will.

They passed the butcher's where Velina had been sent to get the best cuts of meat for Eghrŭn's table and, on rare occasions, buckets of scraps for the workers. They passed the wagonwright's, where the workhouse had sometimes loaned out workers to make adjustments on their most disgusting carriages. And then there was the workhouse.

The corner where they now stood was the very place she'd had the conversation with the traveling tinker that had saved her life. Where she'd traded her last meal for a scrap of paper with a map to the witch's cottage on it—*her* cottage, the place she truly belonged.

She tipped her chin up. She wasn't the same girl she'd been when she'd stood on this corner last. She squeezed Will's arm and dropped the flap of the bag, slipping her hand inside the pocket with the dagger.

"It's there," she said, nodding at it. "They're both in there."

Before Will could put up a fight about Velina getting any closer to the workhouse—his arm had clamped down on hers painfully—they were spared any decision-making by the appearance of a towering orc stomping out the front door.

It was almost comical, how the orc's head turned automatically to scan the street, and how he froze when his gaze landed on the three of them standing on the corner, Velina in the middle, her head held high. What was *not* comical, however, was the disturbing grin that lifted the corners of his lips around his fangs. The hollow pit that had opened up in Velina's stomach at the sight of the workhouse now ached something fierce as the familiar fear tried to take over. But she wouldn't let it. She couldn't. The girls needed help.

Velina's throat had sealed shut. How did she even address the orc? Master. Sir. Eghrŭn. She didn't want to afford him a single courtesy.

"*You,*" she called, her muscles clenched all over. She felt braver than she should with only a muddy street between them, but Finlowe and Will on either side of her gave her courage. "You have two women you shouldn't have, and you'll let them go immediately."

A nasally guffaw erupted from the orc's mouth, and Will straightened up.

"That's not how it works, fae-*blight*," Eghrŭn called. Velina could see one of the orc's enforcers in the shadow of the door behind him. "You belong to me, and so does anyone else under my roof. But I see you have some new friends. I hope they're rich enough to buy out your contract, little blighter."

Will let go of Velina's arm and cleared his throat.

But Velina put a comforting hand on his arm.

"No," she murmured. "Wait."

Fear and concern were painted across Will's eyes, but he gave her the slightest of nods, and she took one step closer to the workhouse.

"No," she said loudly. "We'll not be paying you anything. If you know what's good and right, you'll hand over the girls now."

Her courage mounted as she saw faces peering from the nearby tannery. One or two people actually came out of the alehouse to watch the altercation. Two of Eghrŭn's enforcers slipped from the shadowy alley by the alehouse, watching.

Eghrŭn grunted. "I've had enough jests this day, girl. Get inside. You know what's coming to you for what you've done."

Velina took two steps forward. More faces appeared in windows all over the street; some of the workers even risked the rod by piling at the windows. Velina saw a familiar blonde girl, and she nodded.

"Fine," Velina said. Eghrŭn gave another nasty grin when he thought she was finally acquiescing, but she continued, "You give me no choice. You could have handed them over, the two girls you took illegally." This last part she was practically shouting.

Eghrŭn lowered his voice to a growl. "You think anyone around here cares about that, do you? Think you'll get the Drĕgsons' magistrate involved or somefin'?" He chuckled, his lip curling around his fangs as he shot a conspiratorial glance at one of the men who'd stepped out of the alehouse. Velina recognized him as one of the magistrate's men who was admittedly in Eghrŭn's pocket.

She narrowed her eyes in victory. "Considering one of the girls is Merrylyn *Ravenson*, yes, I do quite think the Drĕgsons and the magistrate will care that you're illegally scooping up workers all over their city."

The magistrate man's face went ashen, and he cocked his head to Eghrŭn, shoving his ale mug at his friend. He strode over, dark brows furrowing on his dark face. "That true, Eghrŭn?"

Velina pointed up at the window where Rhymeris peered out, her arm around a slight girl who only came up to Rhymeris's shoulder. She had a round face with wide, golden eyes that matched her brother's, and pale blonde hair. Not the silver-blonde of someone with faerŭn heritage, but Eghrŭn had likely written it off as *close enough*.

A triumphant look on Rhymeris's face, she pulled Merrylyn from the window and they disappeared from view for a moment. Will and Finlowe came forward to join Velina in the street, while the magistrate man approached Eghrŭn.

"Gerune, the faerŭn girl speaks lies," Eghrŭn said confidently. "She ran away, and now, she is merely trying to trick her way out of her sizeable debt."

Velina put a hand on Will's arm; he gripped it back fiercely. *Sizeable debt, my leg,* she thought. *Being an orphan baby and needing to eat shouldn't be a crime.*

"Then explain that to Will Ravenson and his sister,"

Velina announced. Rhymeris and Merrylyn appeared in the doorway, and Eghrŭn leapt back as if scalded by their presence.

Will rushed to his sister, throwing an arm around her and leading her away from the workhouse door. "You'll be hearing from the Drĕgsons and the Ravensons," Will called to Eghrŭn, not deigning to speak to the slimy orc further. Then he turned to the magistrate's man, "Sir Gerune is it? Keep an eye on this orc. The Drĕgsons will want to speak to him directly about closing his illegal operation and properly housing those under this cursed roof."

Velina's chest swelled, and her eyes watered at the mere idea. She flung her arms around Rhymeris, and the tears broke loose with abandon. She didn't care who saw them. Her tears were a mark of joy, a mark of victory, and a mark of freedom.

17

The next morning, the five of them set out on foot from the Drĕgsons' manor. The noble family had offered them a carriage or horses to speed their journey, but Will had turned them down with a covert smirk at Velina. They only had to walk to the edge of the wood.

Merrylyn had gotten a good night's sleep in one of the manor's many plush featherbeds, after falling asleep in her brother's arms while they relayed their story to Ablenik Drĕgson, the patriarch of the holding. To Velina's surprise, the elder Drĕgson was interested in her own stories of the workhouse—and not only Eghrŭn's but others she'd suffered in.

"The orc's enterprise is over," Drĕgson stated. "And he's in custody. I've also fired the magistrate's enforcers in West Drĕghold who allowed this behavior to continue. Not only the kidnapping and forced labor, but money laundering, tax evasion, illegal vïloil dumping... Though, those aren't as serious," he added with a cringe at the look on Velina and Rhymeris's faces.

After the patriarch promised to look into *all* the workhouses in his city and open communication with the other nobles of Viridia about the pestilential places, Velina practically skipped out of the city's gates, arm in arm with Rhymeris, with Finlowe on the girl's other side. The self-proclaimed thief looked immeasurably glad to leave the Drĕgson estate, where he'd no doubt snooped previously for the faeryn rod before realizing it was at the conservatory.

The Darkwood was in sight, and Will walked ahead, quietly explaining to Merrylyn why they had turned down the offer of a carriage. The younger girl kept throwing incredulously excited glances over her shoulder at the two hooded faerŭn girls.

"You didn't tell me how you got captured by Eghrŭn," Velina said to her friend, nudging her with her elbow. "I knew you shouldn't have gone into West Drĕghold."

Rhymeris appeared to be smothering a smile.

"What?" Velina demanded.

"I didn't get captured," she said with a shrug, letting the smile loose. "After spending only a few minutes in that part of the city, I'd already heard the rumors of the workhouses scooping up more workers. I thought it likely I'd find Will's sister that way."

Mouth gaping open, Velina stared at her. "You did *what*? Why? Even if Merrylyn was taken, you didn't know which workhouse..."

Another shrug rolled off Rhymeris, and Velina walked on, shaking her head. "You're a wonder, you know that?"

A lyrical laugh filled the air. "As are you, my friend. I'm proud of you for confronting the orc. You didn't know if that would work."

Velina swallowed. She hadn't known. And it had only been pure luck that someone from the magistrate's office had been nearby. Though she'd hoped the onlookers would have given her enough support to bully Eghrŭn with the truth.

They reached the edge of the Darkwood; Velina spied the skull rock and the cottage just past it. She was glad it didn't make them wander around three times as it sometimes did. She eyed the crooked door, and her heart leapt. Home.

"Merrylyn, we have to make a quick stop before we get you home," Velina announced, holding the door open for everyone. Finlowe was grinning as he followed Rhymeris into the cottage. Merrylyn smiled nervously, allowing Will to lead her in. "Have you ever been to Elody?"

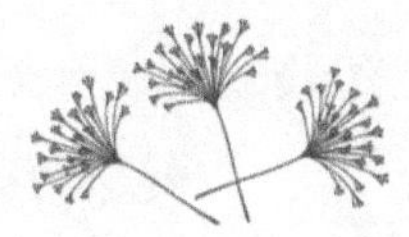

Velina leaned back in her chair on the front porch as she watched the two Ravensons by the edge of the water. Merrylyn had shucked up her skirt high enough to reveal her knees and tucked the ends into her belt, while she splashed in the sea. Will stood with his arms crossed nearby, enjoying watching his newly returned sister with joy, but as hesitant as ever to get wet sand on any part of his body. Velina grinned.

"I miss this cottage," Rhymeris said throatily as she came out of the cottage door in a new outfit, a full scarlet silk dress with a sleek black hood that trailed all the way down her back when not up over her hair.

"Omens," Velina said, eyeing the dress. "How did you get the cottage to give you *that*?"

"Practice," Rhymeris said, perching on another chair on the porch. Finlowe made an appearance in the doorway, leaning against the doorjamb. He was dressed in an equally sleek outfit of red and black.

"You two look like nobles," Velina said. "But Rhymeris, if you miss it here, are you sure you want to leave? I still don't know why *anyone* would ever want to leave the cottage."

Rhymeris sighed and brushed imaginary dirt off her ankle, which she'd crossed primly over her knee. "The stationary life is not for me," she said.

"But—"

"I know. The cottage isn't stationary," Rhymeris said with an eyeroll. "But it has its limitations. It can't leave Viridia. And the building's actually quite tiny, once you've lived in it for a while—and no, you can't make it any bigger. I tried." Velina stared at her. She supposed, much like the broken door, the cottage resisted change.

"I know it's hard to understand," Rhymeris

continued. "And like I said, I miss the cottage sometimes. Maybe all the time." She was quiet for so long Velina thought she wasn't going to continue. The three of them stared at the waves rolling in and out as if the ocean was breathing.

Finally, Rhymeris went on. "You like helping people, I can see that in you. And I do too. But I also want to see the world. Even though the cottage is powerful, it can't bring me past these shores. After being trapped in a life I couldn't control for so long, the cottage gave me freedom. But now I want to try doing something new with that freedom."

"Where do you want to go?" Velina asked in a hush. She'd never heard of anyone crossing the seas before, only vague rumblings about tea from Malchria or bread made from an Imminian recipe. Did people ever come back from overseas?

"I'd really like to find out more about our heritage," Rhymeris said quietly. Finlowe came over; he put a hand on the woman's shoulder, squeezing it.

"That's why I was searching for the faeryn rod," Finlowe said with a knowing wink at Velina. "It was a gift for Rhymeris."

The older faerŭn looked up at him. "You could have told me. I would have helped you retrieve it had I known what it was. Stolen by the Drĕgsons from the faerŭn museum in Villikry, you said?"

"Aye, a lot of faerŭn history there," Finlowe said, nodding. "And as a faerŭn yourself, I reckoned you should have it instead of it being displayed in a glass case in a museum no one goes to."

Rhymeris chuckled. "And I'm sure you *only* wanted it for noble reasons, and not because you heard it could point you in the direction of anything you wanted, right?"

Finlowe simply grinned at her, a twinkle in his eye. "The younger of the Drĕgsons took it in the first place," he went on. "And once he realized it was nothing but a piece of pretty metal, he donated it to the conservatory, which was much easier to...acquire it from."

"I knew you were in there," Velina said in mock accusation. "You're just lucky Merrylyn went missing *before* that happened. I can't believe she was only going for a walk when Eghrŭn's men abducted her. She was hardly anywhere near West Drĕghold."

She watched the girl playing in the water; Will had retreated even farther up the beach after his sister tried splashing him a few times. They had promised the girl some time by the sea before returning her directly to Ravenshold. Finlowe, of all people, had offered to return the horse on foot—after whatever escapade he and Rhymeris were heading to dressed so finely.

Finlowe shook his head. "At least the Drĕgson patriarch will be cracking down on the workhouses in his city now. Should even things out. Maybe the workers will get to see some finery in their lives now. Or at least, livable accommodations and wages."

"That conservatory really was fine." Velina turned back to Rhymeris. "I don't blame you for wanting to travel the world."

The girl smiled a feline grin. "Maybe someday you'll want to too. But I'm happy knowing that you're the witch at the edge of the wood now. As long as you don't mind me stopping by for a new outfit when I return from my travels." Velina smiled, warmth filling her core.

Finlowe slipped the faeryn rod from his vest pocket and handed it to Rhymeris. She held it in her flat palm, which laid upon her scarlet-clad lap.

"I wish I knew the way to Villikry," she said.

The rod spun, pointing straight out across the ocean.

ACT III
THE
WAY

One month later

"I wish my friends were here," Velina said, setting down her empty teacup in the kitchen. For once, the cottage did not make her wish magically appear—that only worked on *things*, as she knew very well by now. Silverweed glared at her with his baleful stare from where he lounged on the back of the sofa, as if offended.

"Of course you're my friend too," she said, coming over to scratch behind his ears. He bumped her palm with his nose in return. She sighed, glancing around the witch's cottage and spotting her broom.

"Maybe I'll go explore Elody," she told Silverweed idly. But what was the point of being the witch at the edge of the wood if she wasn't in the cottage?

So she sighed and grabbed the broom and opened the heavy, half-broken door, leaving behind the scent of fermenting ffrey root coming from her workstation by the hearth. She'd have to strain it in an hour, or it would taste horrible. The waves of the Viridian Ocean greeted her, and she smiled at the expanse of water before she got to work sweeping the porch. She had a few patrons around these parts, so it was possible she'd have some business today.

She had a respectable number of returning patrons now that she'd been purposeful in her ministrations as the witch. Rhymeris and Finlowe had been gone a month now, and Velina only just felt like she was getting the hang of it. Her patron in Fehrgarde who needed the concoction to quiet background noises paid her a hefty sum for a bottle every week, and her blackfork tincture had become her other go-to recipe. Both of those brought in a staggering amount of coin, the likes of which she had never seen before in her life. But what did she need so much coin for? Besides the food she ventured from the cottage to procure, the place provided her with everything she needed. Except company.

Will was having problems with one of his beehives and had to spend extra time tending them; but they still made sure to meet up once a week outside Ravenshold when Velina brought the cottage to the edge of the Ingwood on Myrsday mornings. Some mornings, he brought Merrylyn with him, and the three of them had tea together. Will had supplied Velina with enough honey from his bees to last a lifetime at this point, and Velina always provided the tea—or rather, the cottage did. Merrylyn usually asked Velina to bring the cottage to Elody; the younger girl delighted in frolicking on the beach. Velina didn't blame her. It was where she spent the majority of her time when she wasn't meeting patrons in other parts of the country.

Her stack of coin grew, and so did her guilt, so each week she gave a large portion to Will to donate to the poor in various cities. But her once a week standing tea engagement did little to pass the rest of the time. She spent hours alone in the cottage grinding up herbs or steeping concoctions.

She had asked Rhymeris why she shouldn't just ask for the finished concoctions straight from the cottage, and not just the raw ingredients. The older girl had gone on about the quality of what you were providing for the patron—and the questionableness of giving someone a tincture or salve crafted by a magic cottage. If you didn't ask for it in *just* the correct way, you never knew what exactly was in the jar of liquid or salve that magically appeared. Was the ffrey root fermented long enough to be effective? Had the jusleaf been ground just right to avoid the nasty headaches the leaf spines brought on? There was no way of knowing.

Asking the cottage for raw ingredients and then crafting the potions herself was a better way to ensure that Velina didn't accidentally poison anyone. And though she couldn't ask the cottage directly for food, she found it wouldn't even provide ingredients if they were fresh. Sure, she could ask it for tea leaves or dried bilberries, but it wouldn't conjure up fresh bilberries. She wasn't sure she understood it, but foraging in the Ingwood and purchasing ingredients at the local markets was a delight anyway.

After the porch was free of sand, she rearranged the small table and chairs she kept outside when the cottage was stationary. Then, she perched on the edge of the porch, feet dangling over the sand, staring idly at the waves for a few minutes.

Finally, she made up her mind. She tucked the broom back inside the cottage and swapped it for her sandals, which she carried across the sandy beach. She would go into Elody for a little while and come back when it was time to decant the ffrey root.

She gave the cottage a glance over her shoulder as she meandered out from under the palm trees that shaded her cottage. Her concern that it might disappear and not come back had faded but still lurked in the back of her mind.

At least Silverweed was in there, she thought with a smile. And Rhymeris had told her the cottage seemed to know when it had an owner.

At the thought of Rhymeris, she glanced farther down the beach, far past the small boardwalk, where one lone passenger ship now sat at the Elody docks. The fishing ships were already out for the day. The docks where were Velina had said goodbye to her faerŭn friend and, of course, the roguish Finlowe. They had departed straight for Villikry in search of answers about the faerŭn. Velina was curious herself, but by all the gods and Omens, she would never be curious enough to set foot on one of those massive ships. She happily awaited news from Rhymeris and tried not to worry too much about the girl. Intrusive thoughts of ships going down in a storm often pervaded her mind when Velina saw any of the massive vessels. She shuddered and looked away from the port.

The first shop to greet her was Quincy's Creams, the bakery she frequented on an almost daily basis. But she had already been in there that morning, so Velina only lifted her hand in greeting to the shop owner's daughter who was waving enthusiastically from behind the counter and kept walking. She had no need of additional pastries. As she considered her next meal, she decided she should cook up the potatoes and salted venison she had in the cottage before they got another day older.

The next shop was vacant, dust on the inside of the glass windows, and cobwebs laced over the shelves and cabinets lining the inside walls. Then there was a dress shop, its vibrant hues and flowing gowns attempting to make up for its gray neighbor. The mannequins outside were dressed in outfits Velina thought Rhymeris would like: tight bodices and silky skirts. Velina preferred simpler tunics and leggings or soft cottony dresses with pockets. And of course, her hooded cowl.

She reached up and made sure it was in place as the dressmaker propped open her door and took a lusty breath of air. "Good day to ya!" she cried. "Want to try anything on, my dear? I've got a mirror in the back and can show you how to adjust the skirts!"

"Oh, no," Velina deflected. "I'm not in need of anything."

"*Need's* different than *want*, my dear!" she called after Velina's retreating back.

Velina smiled and continued down the boardwalk, peering into a shop that sold traveling trunks—from massive leather and wood steamer trunks to small hatboxes—then the small tavern, and finally, a bookshop.

She had known the bookshop was here since Will and Merrylyn had dragged her down the boardwalk a few times, but since Velina's reading lessons kept falling to the wayside, she could only admire all the pretty covers. The last time the two Ravensons had ventured down the boardwalk with her, Velina had poured over a leatherbound atlas, her fingers roving over maps of Viridia and beyond while Will and Merrylyn looked up books on beekeeping and music, respectively. What Velina really wanted to explore, however, were the books with stories. She longed to open the pages of a book and lose herself in another world, another time, if only for a moment. Growing up at the workhouse, some of the older kids would tell the little ones stories on dark nights to help them fall asleep; even when she got older, Velina stayed up to listen to them. Stories of gentle ogres, of long sea voyages, and even wicked witches.

The door to the bookshop was propped open, and the bookseller had his nose in a book behind the counter. There *were* some pretty covers peering at her from here, though, so she decided it wouldn't hurt to look around.

The lack of interest from the bookseller affirmed that decision. Velina had been worried that without having Will and Merrylyn here as a buffer, the bookseller might demand to know what book she wanted, and she imagined having to admit that she could not, in fact, read any of them yet. But the bookseller merely turned another page in his book, and Velina meandered down the first aisle of the shop, her fingertips brushing the spines of the books, wondering at the possibilities they contained.

The idea of all the information and stories in these books felt almost as magical as her cottage. But she was beginning to think she might need to learn to read from someone else if she wanted to experience them for herself. She just didn't *have* anyone else to ask. She only had about half an hour before she had to get back to her ffrey root, so she left the bookshop with a wistful smile, hoping that someday she'd be able to read one of the books.

Her steps turned melancholy as she trudged back toward the cottage. A loud bang came from inside the bakery as she passed it, and Velina whipped her head around. Fionagh had her hands on her face, her eyes wide in terror, accidentally smudging flour on her cheek.

Velina rushed into the shop. "Are you all right?" she demanded.

"Oh!" Fionagh cried. "I'm fine. I just... I just..." She huffed, and beckoned Velina closer, so she could see behind the counter. "I just dropped a whole tray of *silvluets*—you know, the ones that deflate if they're handled too harshly."

"Oh, I'm sorry," Velina said, leaning over the counter and staring down at the remains of the multicolored little cakes. The tops had been glazed in maroon and yellow icing, with little designs on each one. But instead of the normally puffy circles they usually resembled, each one was now as flat as a puddle.

"It's all right," Fionagh said, shaking her head. "I was rushing, and when I rush, I ruin things."

"How come you're rushing?" Velina couldn't help the question from slipping out. She'd seen only one other person on the boardwalk the entire time she'd been out here—someone who didn't work in one of the shops, anyway.

It dawned on Velina that Fionagh was friendly enough; she might possibly be someone Velina could ask to help her learn to read. That is, if Velina wanted to admit to the girl that she *couldn't*.

Fionagh's face flushed, and her gaze flicked back to the pastry puddles on the tray on the floor. "Oh, it's just I'm the only one here this week. My father's gone to Ravenshold where we have some family."

Velina's hopes fell. If she had to do all the baking, Fionagh would be much too busy to help her read— now was certainly not the time to ask her. "I have a friend in Ravenshold," Velina said instead. "He comes for tea every Myrsday."

"Really?" Fionagh asked. "That's a far ride to make every week! What does your friend do?"

"Oh," Velina said, her face flushing red. "He keeps bees. He—erm—loves riding horses, so he doesn't mind the distance."

"Is that your friend whose horse you had to board here? I've never seen such a beautiful horse! My father had to drag me out of the barn a few times because I was grooming her. But I almost burned the croissants one time," Fionagh said, leaning both elbows on the shop counter and staring at Velina.

"So you're running the shop by yourself?" Velina asked, changing the subject. She didn't really want the girl asking about why they'd had to leave the horse.

"Yes," Fionagh said, "Father's gone to see if his great aunt can afford—Well, he's visiting family, like I said."

"That's lovely," Velina said, taking up the girl's phrase.

Fionagh grinned, then bent down to pick up the tray, and tossed it onto a back counter in disgust. "I'll have to start them over," she sighed. "They're for a customer in town."

"I wish I could help," Velina said. "I'm in the middle of making something at home, though, and I have to get back. I don't have many customers myself right now, either." She bit her lip. This was the most she'd talked to the girl—to anyone outside of her very small circle of safe friends.

"Oh?" Fionagh asked, again perching her elbows on the counter to stare at Velina. "And what is it that you do?"

"I—um—sell herbal concoctions and salves and the

like from my cottage."

"Really?" she asked, eyes wide. "Where's that, anyway? I know all the places in town."

Velina swallowed nervously. Would Fionagh care if she was a witch? Well, she wasn't really. She was merely faerǔn. "A bit farther down the beach. It's kind of hidden in the palms."

Fionagh cocked an eyebrow. "Interesting. No wonder you don't get many customers! Have you ever thought of moving up here? The shop next door is vacant." The girl waggled her eyebrows at her.

A chuckle escaped from Velina. "No, erm, I don't know, I hadn't really thought of that. I don't think I have much time to attend a *whole* shop."

"You could try setting up some here in the bakery!" Fionagh burst out. "What's your most popular item? We could put a little stand by the door. We would take a portion of the sales, but you could see if people up on the boardwalk are interested. A dwarf used to sell her soap here, before she moved to Fehrgarde. What do you think?"

"Erm—" Velina began. Actually, it wasn't a bad idea, but it was all happening so fast. She could stay in her cottage but have an excuse to come up to Elody more often and get more patrons. "My relaxation tincture is my biggest seller, but it's priced quite high..." That had been Rhymeris's idea. If Velina priced it too low, people would think it didn't work. Velina felt bad taking money from people for anything, considering the cottage gave her almost all of the ingredients—

which was why she donated most of it to the poor.

"Brilliant! You should bring some up. I can help you make a display even. I do all the displays for the pastries. When I'm not dropping them, anyway."

Velina chuckled nervously. "Maybe you can set up the stand, and I'll handle the glass bottles."

"Foot cream?" Fionagh asked, handling one of the globe-shaped jars. Velina gently swiped it from her to replace it on the shelf.

"Trust me," she told the girl. "It works wonders. Actually, why don't you take one?"

Fionagh eyed the price card she had penned—Velina had dictated all the prices, claiming her handwriting was atrocious—and shook her head. "No, I couldn't possibly!"

"I insist," Velina said, shoving the jar back into the girl's hands. "For helping me get more patrons. And besides, you should know the quality of what you're helping me sell."

That night, she set to work brewing up more salves and tinctures. She flipped through *Pepper's Plants and Potions*, the book Rhymeris had earmarked for her. Some of the words on the page popped out at her, but others appeared as strings of completely foreign symbols. She had sworn she used to be able to read the recipe for the cough suppressant cream, but now she couldn't make out half of the ingredients, and her memory failed her. She huffed and flipped through the book for a recipe she could actually read...or at least remember.

The next day she brought the cottage to the wood outside Melodïgha, where she awaited her weekly nerve-calming patron. She spent the rest of her time there brewing up the recipes she knew and bottling various other helpful herbs that could be used on their own.

By the next morning, she was back in Elody with a basket full of salves, tinctures, and oils to deliver to Quincy's Creams. She bade farewell to Silverweed and set off down the beach, nervously adjusting her hair under her hood. She had made up her mind; she was going to ask Fionagh to help her learn to read. It shouldn't be that hard, the girl was perfectly friendly and outgoing.

Checking her reflection in the shop window to make sure her hair was covered before going in, Velina slung her heavy basket higher up on her forearm and yanked the door open.

"Velina!" Fionagh gushed upon spotting her. "We sold *two* of the relaxation jars!" The girl rushed around the counter and threw her arms around Velina, who froze, basket in hand.

She could count on one hand the number of times she'd been hugged in her life, and once again, wasn't sure what to do with her hands. She took her free hand and awkwardly patted Fionagh on the back, getting a handful of the girl's bronze curls.

"I'm so glad," Velina said, pulling away and bringing the basket in front of her as if to ward off any additional displays of affection. "Actually, I have a favor to ask you."

"Anything!" Fionagh said, throwing her arms into the air and bustling back around the counter where she'd been stamping the Quincy's logo onto some paper boxes.

"I...um..." Velina set down the basket on the counter between them. "Well, first of all, I brought some new items, since I had some downtime yesterday."

"And...?" Fionagh asked, eyebrow arched, as she brought down the rubber stamp with a dull *thunk*. "What's the favor?"

"I...was wondering, if you had any spare time—I know you're busy since your father is in Ravenshold— if you might help me learn to read." The words grew quieter and smaller as she spoke.

The rubber stamp went down with one last *thunk*, and Fionagh actually reached out and grabbed Velina's hands—which she had been twisting awkwardly ever since letting go of the basket. "Oh, Velina, of course!"

She pulled them away as politely as she could, then slipped them into her pockets. "Great, that's settled then." She turned to go; her face felt like it had turned as red as the flags they put up on Ferrin's Day each winter.

"Actually," Fionagh started, "we never did decide on the consignment price—you know, for your items?"

"Oh, right," Velina said, whirling around. Somehow

getting back to business drained the heat from her face, and she finagled a fair price for the girl. Fionagh shot down her first offer, insisting "That's *far* too much for the bakery to take!" but eventually they came to an agreement.

"Before I go, I'll take a blackberry pie," Velina said before departing.

Fionagh eyed her suspiciously as Velina handed over most of her cut of the earnings in exchange for the pie. She really didn't need the money. And she might not really need the pie, either, but it smelled heavenly. Surely, she would have at least one slice...so it didn't go to waste. Fionagh packaged it up in one of the boxes she'd stamped earlier, and started to hand it over, but didn't let go of the box.

"When do you want to, you know, meet up to do some reading? Do you want me to come to your cottage? You're coming here all the time to drop off products. It's the least I can do."

"No, no," Velina insisted. "I'll be here anyway, like you said, so it's no bother."

With a shrug, Fionagh finally relinquished the pie box. "How about tomorrow after the morning rush?"

"That would be great." Velina bid her goodbye, a smile tugging at the corners of her lips as she swept out into the salty air.

The scent of vidre flowers and lemongrass pervaded the cottage as Velina finished prepping her calming tonic. She took a deep inhale of the steam as she gave the cauldron one final stir with her wooden spoon.

Silverweed wrapped himself around her ankles as she hung the spoon back on its nail on the hearth. "You could trip me, you know?" she admonished, chuckling as she glanced at the proximity of the fire. "And then, who would feed you?" She reached down and scratched behind his ears, eliciting a soft purr.

She asked the cottage for a new dress, this one green and cream-colored, with deep pockets just the way she liked it. She had gotten the hang of asking the cottage for specific things, but she had also found that the cottage would fill in the details even if she was a little vague. Sometimes it felt like the cottage knew what she wanted better than she did. Donning the hood before she stepped out the broken door, she set off down the beach later than she usually did; she'd waited so Fionagh wouldn't be busy with the early morning patrons.

Velina didn't see much of a crowd by the boardwalk, just a lone old woman storming out of the bakery, deep-set wrinkles furrowed in anger. The cheerful bell tinkled over the door, and Fionagh looked up at Velina in fear, her eyes swimming in tears.

"Wh—Fionagh, what's the matter?" Velina rushed over to the girl.

"I-It's nothing," she said, hastily wiping the tears that managed to escape.

"Who was that woman?" Velina demanded, glancing out at the empty boardwalk. "What did she say to you?" Fionagh was the friendliest person in Elody. Who would have upset her like this?

Fionagh shook her head. "Dowager Marshe owns our building," she said in halting tones. "And she's raised the rent yet again. With less ships coming from Imminia and Villikry, we get nowhere near the amount of traffic we used to, and"—her breath hitched, and her voice went up in pitch—"and my father's trying to secure a loan from his great aunt, but by all the Omens, I don't know if it'll even be enough to last us a few months."

Velina sighed. "Oh." She cast her gaze around the shop as if she might find an answer for the girl, then finally said, "I'm sorry."

Blinking back tears, Fionagh looked up at Velina and gave her a sad smile. "That's why I was excited to help you sell your products here, to help Pa earn some more coin."

"Oh, well, of course," Velina said, clearing her throat. "I've got another recipe brewing back at the cottage now I think people will like. The problem is...I can't read everything in my herbal books." The more she spoke with the girl, the easier it became to admit.

"Let me just get these honey cakes in the oven," Fionagh told her. "And we can get started now."

"Are you sure?"

"Sure. Syldays are always slow. Scone?"

"Sure," Velina said with a grin.

Fionagh lifted a section of the counter and invited Velina to the back, making her feel even more guilt for imposing on the girl. But Fionagh had assured her it was all right, especially now that Velina was selling her products in the shop—she practically worked here anyway, the baker had reasoned. They perched on some wooden barstools, and Fionagh pulled out a quill and a large scrap of oddly thin parchment.

"It's leftover from baking," Fionagh told her. "We use it to keep the croissants and such from sticking to the pans."

Velina noticed the uniform pattern of oddly shaped shadows on the paper.

"We use these for scrap paper all the time. To-do lists and the like. Anyway, I thought we'd start from the beginning, since I don't know what you know." The baker's daughter wrote all the runes in a neat line across the top of the parchment paper, saying each one aloud as she did so.

Will had done his best, but he had started with

whole books, reading words aloud to Velina as if she would know them if he repeated them enough. Fionagh seemed a natural teacher and soon had Velina writing the first few runes on the list. The scone on Velina's plate quickly dissipated, only to be replaced by an equally delicious hand pie filled with roast clams smothered in sauce.

"See, you're getting it!" Fionagh called triumphantly after a while.

Velina had painstakingly written out each of the runes in her own hand. She had seen them often enough after staring at the herbal books in the cottage for hours on end, hoping to make some sense of them. She said as much to Fionagh.

"You have to start small," Fionagh told her. "Once you have the basics, you can apply them to bigger things."

Velina smiled. "That's brilliant," she remarked.

A door sounded behind them, and Velina jumped. They turned to see Mr. Quincy arriving through the back entrance. Warm surprise colored his face at the sight of the two of them with their heads together over the parchment paper.

"My favorite customer!" he said, spreading his arms wide. "And my favorite daughter!"

"I'm his *only* daughter," Fionagh said in a mocking undertone to Velina. They chuckled, and Velina stood, feeling all the more awkward for trespassing behind the counter.

"I should get going," she said. "Thanks for the—

er—"

"No, you don't have to go!" Fionagh said. "We're making progress."

Mr. Quincy peered into the nearest oven—ham and cheese croissants—and set down his traveling bag. "Don't interrupt whatever you're doing on my account. I'm pleased Fionagh's made a new friend while I was in Ravenshold."

Velina smiled. She supposed she should count Fionagh among her small group of friends. The girl had agreed to teach her how to read, after all.

He bustled about for a few minutes, catching Fionagh's eye a few times. Fionagh finally inquired, "How did it go?" Velina tensed.

Mr. Quincy ran a hand over his beard and shook his head. "I'm sorry, Fi."

Fionagh nodded faintly, staring down at the parchment she had been sharing with Velina.

Velina stared down at the parchment too and puffed out a breath. "I really do think that's enough for the day," she said.

"Yes, I guess you're right," Fionagh agreed, her voice higher than usual. "Tomorrow then?"

"I can't," Velina said, heart sinking. "Will's coming for tea—it's a whole day thing."

"Oh," Fionagh said, her face falling even further.

"But I'll be by in the morning for some pastries," Velina said, torn at seeing her friend so sad. "And, um—thank you. For teaching me." She reached over and squeezed the girl's hand.

Fionagh's face brightened. "Of course. I'll see you in the morning then."

"How's the new queen?" Velina asked, tipping back in her rocking chair a little and eyeing the stack of books on the table beside her.

Will crossed his foot over his knee and sighed. "All right. The beginning is tricky though, introducing a new one to the hive."

"I can't even imagine," she admitted. "You'll need to take some of these muffins home, by the way. I'm becoming friends with the girl at the bakery in Elody, and she gave me *way* more than I paid for."

Will picked at the one he'd chosen and grinned. "I'm sure Merrylyn will gobble them up. I swear she's grown half a foot in the last month."

Velina shook her head, then hopped to her feet. "Omens, I've got to take this mirafoil off the fire, I almost forgot."

She bustled about, straining the leaves out of the pot and placing them in a glass jar that appeared in her hand. *I wish I had a tray.* A wooden one appeared on her little worktop by the hearth. Then she asked the cottage for a dozen little jars with glass droppers, which she proceeded to fill up with the liquid from the cauldron.

"That's quite a lot of potions," Will said easily. "Who's come asking for so much?"

Velina's face brightened. "Oh, actually, the bakery is helping me sell my wares in Elody."

"Really? That's great. Then you don't need to spend so much time in the cottage, right? Maybe we could go take in a symphony in Ravenshold!"

"Hmm, I suppose I could get out more. Not that I need the money for the potions. I just like..."

He smiled. "Helping people," he supplied. "But you're allowed to help yourself too, you know."

Insides filling with warmth, she nodded, her silver hair slipping over her shoulder. She wondered idly what Fionagh would think if she ever found out that Velina was faerŭn. The warm feeling in her stomach chilled a little, and she got back to filling her jars.

"Oh, there's going to be a wedding in Ravenshold in the coming month," Will said, effectively dropping oil into the fire.

"What?" she demanded, jaw dropping. "*Please* tell me you had a say in it this time!"

A guffaw burst from his mouth, and he shook his head, his eyes alight with mischief. "No, not me. Omens, no. I think I've finally convinced my parents that I have no desire to marry *anyone*. No, it's my eldest sister Lillyan."

"That's lovely news, provided everyone makes it to the wedding feast on time," she said with a sly smile.

"The two of them seem so smitten, I'll make sure of it myself. Anyway, you're invited, as a friend of the family."

"Really?" she gasped. "I've never even dreamed of attending a wedding before. What am I supposed to wear?"

"I'm sure the cottage will help you," he said, the look on his face a clear indication that he didn't know either.

She glanced fondly about the place. Of course. "What do you think Lillyan would like for a wedding gift?"

He snorted. "I'll ask her. *Dear sister, if you could make a wish for any item you wanted in the world for a gift, what would it be?* And then, of course, I can claim it came from both you and me." They fell into a fit of giggles, picking apart their muffins and sipping tea with honey while Velina finished her concoction.

A few students from the medical college in Fennryswood had happened upon the cottage a few weeks ago, and she knew most of them were coming up on exams soon. Velina had found the recipe in *Pepper's Plants and Potions*, the book Rhymeris had earmarked for her. It only had a few ingredients, and she had deciphered the recipe from the many illustrations on the page. She had found most of what she needed in the jars in her kitchen, but foraged for fresh dew weed herself, because the leaves always made the cottage smell nice.

The last time Velina had made the concoction for the students, one of them had returned with a hen as her way of saying thanks for the long nights of studying made a little easier. Velina had snuck the hen back to the edge of the village of Fennryswood, since she preferred to purchase her meat now that she had money.

She'd decided to make the concoction to bring to the

bakery. Fionagh had seemed quite excited about the whole enterprise, and her enthusiasm was contagious. Besides, it would help the Quincys earn more money to keep their shop open longer.

"Tell me about the girl at the bakery," Will said, leaning back and gazing at her expectantly.

"I don't know, she's nice. Fionagh's—erm—helping teach me to read a bit more too."

His face fell, and he said, "I'm sorry, Velina. I promised to help you, and I—"

"You've been busy with your hive and everything else," she said. "I understand, Will, truly. And besides, you know I love keeping the cottage in Elody. Plus, I get free pastries, apparently."

"She does sound nice. I don't blame you for staying in Elody half the week now. The boardwalk is a nice little area too." Then his face lit up. "Hey, I saw a vacant shop when we were there last. Is it still available?"

Her expression scrunched, she asked, "I think so, why?"

He glared at her. "You're letting the bakery sell your wares. Why don't you just open a shop there on the boardwalk!"

She opened and closed her mouth a few times. "I—well, I don't know if I could handle that all by myself. And what about the cottage?" She could never even *dream* of leaving this place.

"Make everything here and sell it there!"

She twisted her mouth into a frown. "But running a shop all alone, all the time? I don't know, Will. I like it here. I get to sit by the fire and drink tea whenever I want and go wherever I want. And I don't actually need the money. The bakery needs it more, really," she muttered.

He shrugged. "Fair enough. It was just an idea."

But the idea rolled around in Velina's brain all night, even after she deposited Will back in the Ingwood outside Ravenshold. Late that night, after she'd finished bottling the concentration concoction and packed most of the jars into a basket to bring to the bakery, her brain was still whirling. Fionagh and her father really were quite nice. Velina knew what it was like to have no money and an uncertain future. But she doubted she could give them a sum of money like she was donating to the poor through Will.

Silverweed, who had fallen asleep on the rug before the hearth, gave her a sleepy meow as she swept by the fireplace to deposit the basket by the door for the morning. She yawned, idly thinking, *I wish there was a way to help the bakery.*

And then, she had an idea.

Velina woke earlier than usual and found Silverweed warming her feet under the blankets. She extricated herself carefully so as not to wake him and made her way down the ladder to the kitchen nook. After heating the kettle on the hook over the fire, she used it to fill up the teapot.

While the brew steeped—tea leaves and dried hora peels—she looked down at her sleeping clothes and did some thinking. It took her a while to carefully craft a request to the cottage, but eventually, she stood dressed in an elegant version of her outfit from the previous day. With a green hood and collar, the dress leaned closer to the styles offered by the shop on the boardwalk, those Velina thought noble women would wear. Fluffy cream skirts folded amid the green cloak, high belt around her waist, and shiny black boots laced up to her knees.

Then she settled into the small window nook in the kitchen to sip her tea, staring through the clouded cottage window. It was always her favorite part of the day.

She loved the ease with which she could rise out of bed whenever she wanted, choose what to eat—as long as she went out to procure it—and best of all, the tea. Never in all her years in the workhouses had she been able to sleep in, choose her clothes or food, or drink tea while it was still warm. The best she'd gotten were cold dregs the kitchen maids left out.

She closed her eyes, letting out a deep sigh. *Thank you*, she thought to the cottage, as she often did in moments like these. Now, it was time to offer aid to someone else.

She left the cottage, basket in hand, and wove her way up the beach and to the boardwalk. Elody proper spread out far behind the little boardwalk, and being located at the far edge might be why the bakery was suffering. It didn't help that there were fewer ships these days—Velina had heard something about marauders between Viridia and Imminia—but they also weren't getting as much local traffic as they should, either. She was going to change that.

She marched up the boardwalk and past the bakery, hoping to avoid Fionagh's notice. When she reached the empty shop next door, she yanked down the small piece of parchment tacked to the door. It had a local address scrawled on it, and read:

For rent. Inquire with Dowager Margarite Marshe.

Velina continued down the boardwalk, so she didn't have to pass by the bakery again, though now she regretted hauling her potion bottles with her. She ducked down the street at the end of the boardwalk, pleased to see the clean cobblestone streets and the houses lined with flowerboxes at the windows. Elody really was a place of joy—no wonder all the traveling tinkers spoke so fondly of it. She was beyond grateful to have the cottage and the ability to live on the outskirts of this place.

It didn't take her long to track down the address on the parchment. Dowager Marshe lived in one of the largest, cleanest, and most elegant houses in all of Elody; the house wasn't hard to spot once she reached the center of the village. A doorman welcomed her into the foyer, and Velina had to work at keeping her jaw from dropping. The ceilings soared, the chandeliers sparkled, and the marble gleamed, but the walls and decor held little charm. It was as grand a building as even the Ravensons' estate but lacked warmth.

It wasn't long before the doorman returned. He guided Velina to a sitting room where the dowager was perched on a plain maroon chair with a high back.

"What is it?" the woman demanded.

Velina twisted her mouth into a wry smile. "I've come about the vacant store on the boardwalk."

The dowager looked her up and down, and Velina shifted, wondering if the dowager could see through her cottage-provided finery to the faerŭn girl from the workhouse underneath. But evidently, she passed muster under the steely gaze. "Yes, I've been trying to rent it for years now. It's a lovely location," she added defensively, as if passing judgment on anyone who didn't want to rent it.

I wonder if that's why she's raising the Quincys' rent, Velina thought, *since she's been losing the income from that one.*

"I'd like to *buy* it," Velina said, pulling a heavy velvet pouch from her dress pocket. "*And* the bakery next door."

It felt as if a school of tiny wriggly fish had moved into Velina's chest as she approached the bakery, her basket of bottles slung over one arm and a fistful of parchment in the other. But as her foot hit the first step up to the boardwalk, panic seized her. What in all the gods and Omens was she doing? What if the Quincys had made other plans? What if they had already decided to close the bakery? She barely even knew Fionagh and her father.

Breath coming fast, she tried to slow her rapid heartbeat as she nervously made her way up to the bakery door. There were two Elody girls in the shop, each clutching a bakery box and speaking intently over in the corner where Velina's medicinals were displayed. Velina swallowed the lump in her throat and went inside.

Fionagh's face was flushed from the heat of the

ovens, and she called, "Look, we're all out of the foot cream!"

A fit of giggles burst from Velina, and she glanced over at the medicinal display. "I told you it was good. A recipe from a friend, that one."

The school of fish in her chest seemed to have moved down to her stomach, and she was now wondering if it had been such a good idea to have that leftover slice of blackberry pie for breakfast.

"Father's in the back kneading the dough for the Berdûne buns," Fionagh reported. "We could do some reading once I get the scones out of the oven."

"Oh, um, actually, I have something to tell you." Velina lifted the basket of concentration concoction up onto the counter.

But at that exact moment, two things happened. Mr. Quincy came out from the back room in the middle of stretching dough, holding the blob over his knuckles and pulling in opposite directions. And the front door of the shop opened, revealing Dowager Marshe.

Velina's mouth dropped open. She thought she would have more time before the dowager arrived. The woman must have taken a carriage directly down to the beach.

Mr. Quincy lowered his hands, the genial smile on his face melting into an expression of forced indifference. "I've already given you my notice, Dowager, I didn't think we had any other business together."

The dowager's wizened face twisted into a not-altogether unpleasant smile, and she said, "We don't. A change in business plans, I'm here to report, Mr. Quincy. I'm no longer the landlord of this establishment."

"Y-You're not what?" Mr. Quincy stuttered.

"Yes," the dowager replied idly, her gaze trailing to the medicinal display in the corner and landing on Velina. "You're looking at your new young landlord right here."

Velina pressed her lips together and smiled guiltily at the two Quincys. Fionagh's hands went to her face, as usual getting a little flour on anything she touched.

It didn't take long for the dowager to walk them through the signatures on the fistful of paperwork Velina carried. Under Mr. Quincy's scrutinizing gaze, Velina was assured the dowager had drawn them up properly.

Velina wasn't entirely surprised by the relief that had washed over the dowager's face once the transaction was fully and finally complete. Soon Dowager Marshe was heading for the door. It had all happened so fast.

"One more thing," the dowager drawled. Velina's heart wrenched. Was there a catch? "I'd like to purchase this foot cream I keep hearing so much about all over town."

M r. Quincy muttered something about needing a lie down, a punch-drunk grin on his face as he thanked Velina for the ninth time and disappeared into the back room shaking his head.

Fionagh dashed around from behind the counter and threw her arms around Velina, "Oh, Velina! How could you? *How!*"

"I, um—" She threw her arms right back around the girl, her eyes pricking with joyous tears. She knew then that she'd done the right thing, and that this was her calling, the way to happiness. To help people. But she still had to explain the rest of her plan. She pulled away and saw Fionagh dash away tears of her own.

"There's more," Velina admitted.

"M-more?" Fionagh's voice quivered.

Velina frowned in concentration. "You see, I also bought the space next door, to help sell my medicinals. But I can't be there all the time. I have...other places to be. So I thought—if you and your father agree—we break down this wall and expand the bakery. You could have a little seating area where people can eat right here in the bakery, and on the far wall would be my medicinals. An apothecary wall, if you will. I'd just need you to tend to the purchases when I'm out of town."

Fionagh gaped at her. "I—Really? Expand the bakery?" She shook her head. "Pa and I were *just* talking this morning about how we would have to close and leave Elody... And now, this is...this is wonderful, Velina! How could you possibly..."

"I had the money, and I wanted to help a friend," Velina said, turning away and stocking the concentration concoction on the medicinal display.

Fionagh cleared her throat and said in a low voice, "You must sell a lot of those, to be able to afford *buying* the two shops from the dowager. I—I had no idea."

Velina nodded. "That's why I travel a lot. People all over Viridia come to me for lots of different things."

"Of course," Fionagh said shakily. "Do you—er—want me to write a placard for those new ones?"

"Sure," Velina said, pleased. "Concentration concoction. Some students from Fennryswood inspired it."

"Fennryswood?" Fionagh said, eyes wide. "You really *do* travel."

Velina nodded with a grin.

Tears were in Fionagh's eyes as she gazed around the bakery with what seemed like a new outlook. "I just—*thank you*, Velina, for helping us. You really are a blessing from the Omens."

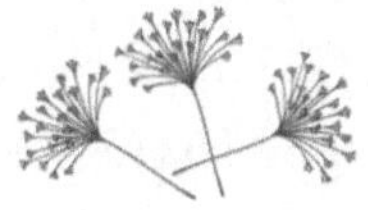

Velina hastened away from the bakery loaded with boxes of sweets that Fionagh had piled on her. A flurry of emotions rallied in her chest, and she wasn't sure what to make of half of them. Gratitude that she had the resources to help the Quincys save their family's business from going under. Nerves at the idea of expanding her potions to an entire half a shop, changing her whole life. And fear...of the Quincys finding out who she really was, which could send the whole thing toppling down.

She burst into the cottage and tried to shut the door behind her without using her full hands, but as usual, the one hinge gave her trouble, and she was left with a crack through which she could hear the ever-present waves.

What was she *doing?* She should have just stayed in the cottage, brewing up "potions" for people who came by. This was bigger than anything she'd dreamed of when she moved into the cottage and became the witch. And Fionagh was a fantastic friend. What if things went sour with the business deals, or the Quincys hated faerŭn like everyone else, and it was all ruined?

Velina bit her lower lip. She might be good at brewing medicinal concoctions, but in truth, she was a deceiver who lied to everyone except Will and Rhymeris. She flung back her hood and stormed over to the kitchen, spooking Silverweed who was lounging on the back of the sofa. He darted up the ladder to the loft, not even deigning to shoot her an annoyed glance.

She set down the pile of pastry boxes on the counter and grabbed the dropper bottle of relaxation tincture she kept for herself. Just as she was pouring a cup of tea to put a few drops of tincture into, she heard a soft knock on the door.

"Omens, what now?" she muttered. But the familiar words seeking the witch didn't come. Through the crack in the door, she spied a slip of familiar bronze hair, and she gasped.

"Hello?" Fionagh called. "Velina?"

Her friend must have followed her here. The cottage did lie at the *edge* of the wood.

"Just a minute," Velina called, setting her hood back over her hair, and bustling back over to open the door. She swallowed when Fionagh smiled up at her, peering curiously behind her at the inside of the cottage, which in truth looked very *witchy*.

"I never knew this was here!" Fionagh trilled.

"Oh, yes, well..." Velina trailed off, gesturing vaguely.

"It's just that, um, I forgot to give you something."

"I *really* think I have enough pastries, Fionagh."

"No, it's—" The girl huffed and pulled a book from under her arm. "This was my mother's. She used it to teach me to read. I want you to have it as a thank you for saving the bakery."

Velina didn't know anything about Fionagh's

mother, except that her picture hung in the back of the bakery, and Mr. Quincy touched the frame every time he walked by.

Mouth agape, Velina shook her head. "I couldn't possibly—"

"Of course you can," Fionagh said sweetly.

Velina swallowed, and her stomach felt cold. Fionagh must have seen something dark in Velina's expression. The baker's grin drooped as she hung her head. "I know I shouldn't have followed you here," she said quietly. "I'm sorry, I'll go—"

"Fionagh," Velina said painfully. "It's not...that." She heaved in a breath. "It's...there's just a lot about me you don't know."

Fionagh threw her hands in the air. "That's it? I thought you were having second thoughts about buying the bakery."

A snort-like chuckle burst from Velina. "There's a lot more to it. I—"

The baker's daughter put her hands on her hips.

Velina stared at her. Fionagh was teaching her how to read out of the goodness of her heart. Would she really care? It was hard to know... All her life she'd been treated like the muck on the bottom of a boot—until she'd met Will. But Fionagh was also her friend, wasn't she?

After a minute, Velina raised shaky hands and pulled away her green hood, revealing her pointy ears and the silver hair she kept bound in a tight braid down her back. Fionagh's face had frozen.

"I'm sorry," Velina said, hanging her head and looking down. "And that's not even all of it." *The cottage, the witch...*

"I couldn't care less what you look like on the outside. And whatever else you've done...do?" She huffed. "Your friend comes from Ravenshold every Myrsday, just for tea? You travel to Fennryswood and Fehrgarde and Melodïgha and still stop by for pastries every morning? I knew there was something..." She waved her hand for Velina to fill in the rest.

Velina wrung her hands, stealing a glance at her friend. Something about Fionagh's expression made her say, "Come inside. I'll show you."

"That doesn't sound ominous at all," Fionagh remarked, following her past the half-broken door. "You should really get someone to fix this."

Velina snorted, shoving the door closed with her shoulder. "Are you sure you want to know everything?"

Fionagh pretended to think about it. "Hmm... Yes. I followed you down the beach and now into your spooky cottage. I think I can handle it."

Despite her nerves dancing like oil and water in a pan, Velina gave her a sly smile, and said, "I wish we were in Ravenshold."

Fionagh gave her a look. "Why? I thought you liked Elody. Well, I guess you have a friend in Ravenshold—" Her rambling stopped abruptly when Velina yanked open the door, the sight taking the rest of the words from the girl's mouth. Fionagh stood there with her mouth half open for more than a minute, then finally whispered, "That's not Elody."

"No," Velina said quietly. She reached up to adjust her hood—she'd forgotten the thing was already off. "I wish I had a new walking stick," Velina said, her voice still low.

"Wh—" Fionagh began. But this time, the result was immediate. A dark wooden stick appeared in Velina's hand, shiny with varnish, comfortably gnarled at the top. Heart racing in her chest, Velina offered it to Fionagh. "Do you want to take a walk?" And for all the gods and Omens, the girl nodded.

When the sun began to descend into the mountains behind Ravenshold, they headed back to the cottage, cloaked in the silence that had prevailed over their entire walk through the Ingwood. Velina thought of it as a nice way to say goodbye. Because there was no way—based on how Fionagh kept glancing at her with wide eyes—that she would want anything to do with Velina after this.

Velina found the cottage, glad that she had that much to rely on, even if it couldn't afford her any company. She would miss her daily visits to the bakery. Perhaps she could just let the Quincys take over the second shop and remain their landlord in name while not spending any time in Elody. That was probably for the best. Fionagh followed her inside, and Velina turned her back on the girl and shut the door as far as it would go.

"I wish we were—"

"It's amazing, Velina," Fionagh warbled.

"I—no, I... What?" Velina blurted out.

"It's magic. *You're* magic. I knew there was something about you!"

Shaking her head, Velina said, "There's something all right. A girl who grew up in workhouses because of my faerŭn heritage and who now deceives everyone she knows—"

"And who has the biggest heart," Fionagh continued, "and who *helps* everyone she knows, I think is what you mean."

"That doesn't—"

"Velina," Fionagh said crossly. "Stop it. I'm not afraid of you. This doesn't change—"

A knock sounded on the door. The hairs on the back of Velina's neck stood up. She'd shut the door. Now, they could be anywhere. She groaned.

"I'm—I'm looking for the witch?" The voice came tentatively from outside.

Fionagh's jaw dropped, but her eyes were filled with anticipation. *"The witch?"* she mouthed, and an expression of joyous understanding washed over her face.

Velina shushed her and tried to direct her to the ladder up to the loft. "Shh! I have to get this, just go—"

"No way!" Fionagh insisted. "I need to see this!"

The patron knocked on the door once more. "Hello?"

Velina's eyes bulged, and she said, "Fine, but put this on—" While speaking, she'd asked the cottage for a black hooded cloak, which she now shoved at Fionagh. The girl eagerly donned it, and Velina pointed near her large wooden table, where the girl parked herself. What in the Omens had she gotten herself into?

To Velina's great relief, the patron was one of the students from Fennryswood. "I just wanted to thank you, Mistress Witch. I passed my examinations—we all did! We knew all the material, but not having the nerves to be able to concentrate fully, well, we wanted to thank you."

Velina looked down at what the girl was offering her and was relieved it wasn't another hen. It was a basket of flowers, gathered from the beautiful countryside of Fennryswood, which Velina could see from the open door. She smiled down at the basket and took it from the girl, whose dark braids swung over her shoulder as she dug something else out of her dress pocket. "And this," the girl said.

It was a small wooden box, which contained three dark brown blobs that smelled somehow sweet. "What...is it?"

"Oh!" the girl said. "It's chocolate. Jarryn's family runs a confection shop here in the village. You should stop by some time!"

After making a vague promise to do so, Velina thanked the girl and sent her off. As she shut the door, she immediately thought about being in Elody and cracked open the door to reveal a sliver of sandy beach. Before she turned back around, she paused for a moment. She had no idea what to expect from Fionagh now that the girl knew the whole of it.

The girl's face cracked into a smile. "I can't believe you hid all of that from me! No wonder you had so much coin to buy the shops! You really *can* go all over the country. And this cottage? How did you get it? How long have you known you had magic?" The questions went on and on, and Velina's mouth dropped farther the longer they went.

"So, you...you're not mad or—or..."

"Velina, anyone who would walk away after finding this out about you is not worth knowing."

A dam broke loose in her chest, and Velina sobbed. Fionagh came over and put a hand on her shoulder, giving it a hearty squeeze.

The cottage had given her respite after almost two decades of hard labor, but now she'd finally found a way to live in her new life, the way she wanted. She could help people, *and* she could have friends and be happy.

Velina gave her friend a watery chuckle. "I bet you were wondering how a girl who couldn't even read could afford all that."

Boards fell to the floor as the workers ripped out another piece of the wall. Velina cringed as they came crashing down, but everything in the bakery was covered in waxed cloth, and the ovens had been off for at least two days already. The workers—recommended by none other than Dowager Marshe when she stopped by for her second jar of foot cream—hauled the pieces away and tossed them into the wagon they'd parked on the beach outside.

Velina grinned and clutched the mug of tea Mr. Quincy had given her. She'd arrived bright and early that morning to help cover everything, and Fionagh had been waiting for her at the edge of the boardwalk with a grin.

"I guess we're really doing this," Velina muttered under her breath.

Fionagh pulled her back outside, where they'd taken to perching on the edge of the boardwalk while the workers destroyed the wall. "Yes, we're really doing this. It was your own Omens-cursed idea, anyway, witch," she added with a wink.

Velina snorted and sank down to the spot she'd claimed on the planks, next to the stack of parchment paper Fionagh had been sketching on, which was weighed down against the breeze by Fionagh's empty teacup. They'd spent the morning going over ideas for the new seating area and the apothecary wall display. Mr. Quincy wandered over every so often to offer his ideas with a pleased smile plastered to his face.

Fionagh had assured her that her father was entirely relieved to be able to simply run the bakery—his lifelong dream—and not have to worry about the finances owed to the dowager. He insisted upon paying rent for his half of the space, but he and Velina had worked out a fair price. She was sinking it all into the renovations and planned to post flyers throughout Elody to announce the grand re-opening.

They watched the workers rip out the boards, leaving four thick vertical support beams in place between the two halves of the new space. When the sun reached the apex of the sky, however, Velina drained her second cup of tea and bid goodbye to the Quincys.

Back at the cottage, she hastened to shut the door behind her and wish herself to Ravenshold, already saddened by the possibility of missing some big development at the shop.

"Hi, hurry!" she called to Will when she spotted him in the Ingwood moments later.

"Merrylyn took forever to get ready," he moaned, shooting a glance back at his younger sister. The scarf that Velina had made for his birthday hung around his neck, but he was already taking it off to stuff in a pocket.

"It's not my fault! Lillyan forced me to go to the seamstress this morning for my gown fitting!"

Velina grinned and ushered them inside the cottage. "Come on, come on."

In no time at all, Velina had returned to the sand and the sea. She inhaled the salty air like it was the finest perfume. Her gaze going up and down Merrylyn, she asked the cottage for a wide-brimmed sunhat and handed it to the girl.

"You were as red as a Ferrin's Day flag last time you came to the beach. I'm not going to answer to Lillyan at the wedding for why you're sunburned again."

Merrylyn donned the hat and stuck out her tongue.

"Wait til you see it," Velina gushed to Will, who hooked his arm in hers as they made their way down the beach.

The wagon outside was piled with lumber, but Velina's heart still leapt upon spotting the little boardwalk storefronts and the people outside them.

But what made her heart leap straight into her throat was the sight of a ship just off the coast. Could it be...? No, Villikry was so far off, and Rhymeris wouldn't possibly be returning to Viridia so soon.

She made formal introductions between the Ravensons and the Quincys before Merrylyn sauntered down to the water's edge, already shucking up her long rose-colored skirts and tossing her shoes onto the dry sand. Velina smiled and began to show Will the construction, along with Fionagh's sketches and even the ideas for new pastries they'd come up with after sampling the chocolate from Fennryswood. He stared at the open wall space, making suggestions for the seating area, getting down onto the planks to sketch his ideas on bakery parchments with the charcoal pencil, and absentmindedly chewing on one of the meat pies Fionagh had brought over.

Velina had all but forgotten the ship arriving at port until she heard footsteps on the boardwalk. She looked up to see a half dozen people meandering around the shops. One pair, however, strode purposefully down toward the end of the boardwalk. Velina looked up from the paper where Will had sketched his rendering of shelving to house all her jars and saw the familiar faces. She surged to her feet and rushed toward the approaching girl, her arms flung wide.

"What are you—? *How are you back already?*" she demanded.

The faerŭn girl smiled slyly at her.

"She missed home," Finlowe said, nudging Rhymeris with his elbow.

"I got answers enough," Rhymeris admitted. "And I missed you and the cottage."

Velina enveloped her in another hug. "I missed you too," she said, speaking muffled words into the girl's silver hair.

"Answers?" Will leaned against one post of the covered boardwalk. "What did you find out?" he asked, lowering his voice.

Velina had her hood up once more; though she'd revealed her heritage to Mr. Quincy the day after she'd told his daughter, she felt it was only right for him to know who he was in business with. His reaction matched Fionagh's, but Velina was still nervous about the other townsfolk finding out.

Rhymeris glanced around at the present company—the workers were busy cleaning up the dust and splinters inside from all the boards they'd ripped out—and murmured, "Lots to tell you, Velina. I saw faerŭn hills and standing stones, met a few others, and my favorite part—I found a legend that says we're descended from elves, not fae of any kind."

Velina raised her eyebrows, one hand going up to touch her ear inside the hood. "Elves? I've never heard of them."

"There was a lot of lore in Villikry," Rhymeris assured her. "I've got plenty to tell you about. And it looks like you have a lot to catch me up on! What in the name of all the gods and Omens is going on in there?"

Velina grinned. "*This* is the beginning of Quincy's Creams and Apothecary."

Finlowe eyed Will's unfinished meat pie hungrily. "I don't suppose you have anything to eat back at the cottage? The ship fare was...ungodly."

Rhymeris chimed in. "I could use a new outfit too."

"Of course," Velina said, her heart warming. "You're welcome to stay as long as you want."

The other faerŭn girl shuddered. "I'm not sure

there's room enough for us in that cottage along with you. We've already spent enough time cramped on that ship."

Velina's gaze darted to the second floor above the new side of the shop. "If you give us some time, I'll have a second living space available soon."

Everyone's gaze followed hers up to the window above the empty part of the shop, and Rhymeris returned her grin with gusto. "You seem to have found your own way, eh, dearie?"

"I sure have."

I wish everything could stay just as perfect as it is now, Velina thought. And though the cottage lay farther down the beach, she had a feeling the chances were high of that wish coming true.

THE END

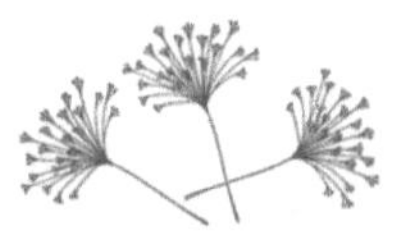

Acknowledgements

This book has been such a joy to put out into the world, and I have so many people to thank for encouraging me along the way. Thank you to my husband Jeff for always supporting me, even if you think a certain character shouldn't have left the cottage... Thank you to Steph, Dave, and Kimberly for the early read and encouragement.

Amy Marchant, thank you for bringing Velina to life for the first time with your illustration!

Thank you to Amber Finnegan for illustrating the cottage scenes and character art!

Sara Lawson, thank you for helping make my writing make sense, and for your love for Will and his bees!

Incredible thanks goes to Deborah Balm, who narrated an amazing audiobook and brought Velina and her friends off the page in the coziest, most fantastic way.

And a **massive** thank you to all the Kickstarter backers who helped support this story and turn it into such a fantastic book. Your support and enthusiasm has been incredible. Thank you:

Jo Anderson
Christy
Christina Jackson
Jasmine Young
Mark Goodfellow
Chase McGlinchey
Sara Lawson
Cara Blaine - Author
Rose
Jeffrey Delton
Amanda Snodgrass
Danesha Beckwith
Cortney
Valia Lind
Carly Arave
Herman Steuernagel
David Trotter
Emily
Katie Cross
Leslie
Ashley Heinzke
Tonour
E.G. Stone
Billye Herndon
Delemhach A.K.A Emilie
Nikota
Natasha Savoie
Elizabeth
Nicole
Krys G
Dave Pergola
Sarah
Melinda Cater

BeeGreen
Scarlett
John Idlor
MichelleG
Natalie MUNFORD
Alexandra Corrsin
Agnes Jankiewicz
Rebekah Margaret Doss
Megan Haskell
MaeNadlen
Thona Bitzer
Gianna Christopher
Gregory Butt
Iris
Dayna
Dead Fish Books
Samantha Landstrom
Samantha Newberry
Megan Astell
Ben Petitt
Catherine Holmes
Olia Baghdanov
KETS
Marlene Renteria
DebMarie Gilmore
Jean Sitkei
David Holzborn
Amanda Balter
Lucy
Dean Lambert
Jenna Minick
Joshua MacDonald

Stefani Stewart

Polina Bazlova

Astrid V.J.

Kelly

Alicia Parczen

Emma

Sarah Reynolds

Ali Finn

Ken Baker

Hazel Thompson

Margaret Beeler

Becky

Stephen Wang

Sam

Todd DeDecker

S.L. Rowland

Sabrina Wierzchowski

Denise Pratt

Michelle Holloway

Jenny Schwartzberg

Connie Moore

Elizabeth Carrillo

Brittani

Lorien Cord

Diane Ottobre

Jean Sylvia

Margaret A. Menzies

Brittany

John P Curtin

Sue Still Author (she/her)

John

Nicola M Wilkinson

lancekrautlarger

Jessica D Hoyal

Adam Nadolsky

Luke G

jessica staub

Jessica Kurnas

Rick Parker

Troy H.

shay dinur

Nikki P

Thomas Bull

Jessica Arden Cline

Richard Earl

Evelyn

Mickey Spencer

Valerie Love

Kenyon Wensing

Tatiana Lightwood

Nathalie

Diana M Blount

Matthew Rohde

Eric Ostby

Katrhiana Bauer

Carol Long

Alexis

Rebecca Godby

ddemarco

Clay

Ly's

Mary Craver

Anne Mollova

Larisa Ignacio

<table>
<tr><td>

Barbara Middelkoop-Meijsen
Crystal_Lilly
Emma Adams
Rhianne | R. S. Williams
Tristan
Nichelle Preston
Katie Warner
Whitney Anderson Beaugh
Neil Houston
Elizabeth Semkiu
Tiffany
Meshia
Matty Colley
Nirkatze
Dakota
Krystal
LaToya Moritis
Canari
Eileen Halecki Corwin
Megan Cooper
R. Lennard
Jennifer Oramous
David Litsky
John 'Jake' Enrique Lyde
kelly k
Marcela Mets
Marvin Travon Turner
Anonymous
Rhiannon McFarling
Jenny O
Sara Francis
Linda Wakefield

</td><td>

Preston Mack
Jeremy Busey
Kayla Maurais
Brittany Colon
Renae
Christy S.
Lori Wolbrueck
Claude Baridon
Walter
John Fritz
Rene Gutierrez
Cat
Lady Magda Sofia
Allyssa Lonergan Day
Jennie
Leslie
Noah S.
Grey
Dave Dehaan
Jojo Rose
Emma Jo Gregory
Katherine Malloy
Charissa Chi
Caroline Sofie
Heather Hyatt
Jojo
Kelsey Thomas
Catherine Leja
Pamela
Jessica
Chumyshka
Nicole Sanders

</td></tr>
</table>

Deirdre Robertson
Edel Moran
Andrew Shell
Carol Gonzales
Sarah Inscore
Mallory
Carl H Spitzer
A E Richardson
Krystal Bohannan
Ellie Brick
Midnightmare
Mustela
Therese Marie Edman
Susan
Michelle L
Melissa
Belwood Publishing
Kim A.
David Bock
Giuliana
Jamie R. Brott
Lycoris

Patty Rau
Liana
Stephanie
Rosa
Lisa
Marina Sanin
Elizabeth Bennett
Louise Wade
Nicole Klein
Antoinetta Aquila
M. H. Woodscourt
Anastasia Lewis
Chris Roeszler
Christine Andres
Kate Nass
Charlotte
Sara Liming
Jan Berčič
Wineke Sloos
A Reece
Rachel

About the Author

Liz Delton writes and lives in New England, with her husband and sons. She studied Theater Management at the University of the Arts in Philly, always having enjoyed the backstage life of storytelling.

World-building is her favorite part of writing, and she is always dreaming up new fantastic places.

She loves drinking tea and traveling. When she's not writing or reading, you can find her baking in the kitchen or out in the garden making valiant attempts at keeping her plants alive.

Visit her website at **LizDelton.com**

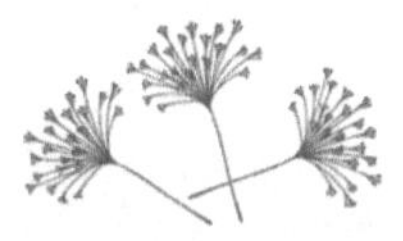

ALSO BY LIZ DELTON

The Witch at the Edge of the Wood

LEGENDS OF GOLD AND SILVER
Flames of Gold
Echoes of Silver

REALM OF CAMELLIA
The Starless Girl
The Storm King
The Gray Mage
The Starlight Dragon
The Fall of Azurite
Realm of Camellia Omnibus

SEASONS OF SOLDARK
Spectacle of the Spring Queen
The Mechanical Masquerade
All Hallows Airship
The Clockwork Ice Dragon
Seasons of Soldark Novella Collection

<u>EVERTURN CHRONICLES</u>
The Alchemyst's Mirror

<u>FOUR CITIES OF ARCERA</u>
Meadowcity
The Fifth City
A Rift Between Cities
Sylvia in the Wilds
The Four Cities of Arcera Omnibus

<u>WRITER'S NOTEBOOKS</u>
Writer's Notebook
Teen Writer's Notebook
Guided Writer's Notebook

Shop **LizDelton.com**
for signed books, merch, and exclusive bundles.